THE BEAST

AFTER ME

The Beast After Me
Copyright © 2021 Beau Lake. All rights reserved.

4 Horsemen
Publications, Inc.

4 Horsemen Publications, Inc.
1497 Main St. Suite 169
Dunedin, FL 34698
4horsemenpublications.com
info@4horsemenpublications.com

Typesetting by Michelle Cline
Editor Vanessa Valiente

Library of Congress Control Number: 2021941798

Print ISBN: 978-1-64450-282-2
Audio ISBN: 978-1-64450-283-9
E-book ISBN: 978-1-64450-284-6

The WOLVES of WHARTON
Book Four

AFTER ME

BEAU LAKE

4 Horsemen
Publications, Inc.

TABLE OF CONTENTS

Prologue
(LEIGH)

◁◆▷

A horse-and-carriage trundles down Decatur Street, the gaslights casting ominous shadows across the equine's visage. It's wearing blinders, and the rectilinear shadows make it appear as though its eye sockets are empty and cavernous. Steam pours from its flared nostrils as it huffs, its hot breath commingling with the unseasonably crisp nighttime air. I watch it until it disappears onto Jackson Square, its braided tail twitching at the unrelenting mosquitos. Despite the chill, the insects are undeterred.

A drunk man lurches past my table, laughing. His cheeks are ruddy, and, like the horse, his breath is a cloudy vapor, making it appear as though his head is seconds from igniting. I can't help but imagine what would happen if he succumbed to spontaneous combustion. His torso would catch fire first, the layer of fat around his midsection acting as fuel, his Misfits t-shirt as tinder. He would freeze midstep, the rubbery soles of his Nikes fusing to the asphalt. He would burn so brightly and with such ferocity that he would be little more than a pair of disembodied feet within seconds. They would never be able to wash his stain off Cafe du Monde's patio.

As usual, the French Quarter is a discordant cacophony, pairing perfectly with my turbulent mood. Jazzy music tickles my eardrums, the syncopated beat of the snare drum thumping deep into my chest wall. All the tables surrounding mine are occupied, and I am privy to several unrelated conversations with one common thread. *I was so drunk last night, I woke up in bed with Jake. Can you fucking imagine? We will have to take an Uber.*

"I brought you something to eat," Luka says, placing a ceramic plate on the table before me. There are three fluffy beignets on the plate, greasy from the deep fryer. The younger man sits in the empty chair across from mine, a steaming mug of café au lait in hand.

"I'm not hungry." I push the plate away with the tip of my finger. Even with the sweet dessert and Luka's chicory coffee on the table, I am convinced I can still smell the Mississippi River slow rolling just beyond the promenade. The river is thick with sediment and reeks of mildew. I can almost taste it on my tongue.

"You look *awful*," Luka observes. He selects a flaky, soft pastry from the plate and takes a bite. Confectioners' sugar clings to his upper lip, making him appear mustachioed.

"Careful," I warn.

"I just mean…you should eat *something*," he clarifies. His eyes flit up and down Decatur Street, still delighted by the sights and sounds after ten months.

Even in our shared apartment blocks from the French Quarter, I often catch him holding the blinds open with his thumb and forefinger, watching the street below.

Someone lights a blunt as they stride past the patio, the skunky, herbal scent tangling around us. "I'm not hungry," I insist.

Luka finishes the first beignet, licking sugar off his long, slender fingers. He has painted his nails black and gold—Saints colors. A gush of affection sweeps through me at the sight of him: so young, so sanguine. He took to New Orleans just as readily as he had Wharton before it.

"You *really* should have one bite," he insists.

I reach into my jacket pocket, pulling out a folded envelope. I've stalled long enough. Luka's bushy eyebrow arches, a question implicit therein. "There's enough cash in here to pay rent for three months," I explain. "Or it's enough for a plane ticket back to Portland, if that's what you would prefer."

Luka doesn't reach for the parcel. So, I place it on the table. "I need to go my own way," I continue, "as a lone wolf."

The look on his face makes me wish I had said anything else. It's as though I had stabbed him in the belly, soaking his pristine Nike Airwalks with his own blood. For an instant, he looks like a child again, his eyes watery and his lower lip trembling.

He coughs into his fist, forcing the emotion out of his chest. "You're going back to Wharton," he says. It's not a question. He must have seen this coming, just like how our neighbor divines the future in her tea leaves. *Watch your step, Leigh*, she'd said, just this afternoon when I saw her hanging her laundry on the line. *It's easy to lose your way if you walk off the trail.*

"I have to," I reply.

"What are you planning?" Luka rests his forearms on the table, leaning close. His breath smells faintly of coffee, and I wrinkle my nose. The redolence of coffee reminds me of my twin brother's neck, bent at an impossible angle. It reminds me of his sightless, staring eyes. It reminds me of my hands, slick with his blood, as I tried to rouse him with soft pats, then by violent slaps. *Wake up, wake up, wake up!*

"It doesn't matter," I reply. "I just don't want to leave you in a tough spot."

"He's gone, Leigh," Luka murmurs. "Nothing you do will get him back." He picks at one of the remaining beignets, tearing it into tiny pieces. Sugar floats in the air like fairy dust. "I loved him too. He and Angus were like my surrogate dads."

Hearing Angus' name is like a fist to the jaw. I haven't said it aloud in months; I'd hardly thought it. Instead, I call him what he is: the murderer. "I know," I manage. "I know you loved him, and I know he can't come back. But my business in Wharton isn't done."

A group of men gather just off the patio, sporting hard-bodied instrument cases. When one is opened, I catch sight of a French horn, its bell reflecting the twinkle lights above Cafe du Monde, the gaslights flanking the street. They'll be playing soon, the familiar melodies of *Iko Iko* and *Little Liza Jane* drowning out everything else.

I'm grateful for it; this conversation will have to end shortly, and I will not have to hear him calling after me when I walk away.

"What are you going to do?" Luka repeated. He reaches for my hand, but I slip away from his grip with a measured twist of my wrist.

"Take care of yourself, Luka," I tell him, rising, tucking my chair back under the small cafe table. As the first mellow, buzzy sounds of jazz fills the air, I lean over and kiss the twenty-year-old atop his head. "Don't follow me," I murmur into his hairline.

He stiffens, keenly aware of the threat layered beneath the adjuration.

I pass the towering spires of St. Louis Cathedral and the card tables covered in silk scarves and Tarot cards before the tears come. "Miss, fancy a reading?" a panhandler calls "Or, I could read that pretty little palm of yours!"

I ignore him; I don't need to see the cards to know my future.

CHAPTER ONE
(HALEY)

———◁◆▷———

She's coming.

Branches slap against my tear-streaked cheeks as I barrel through the tree line, cutting shallow trenches in my flesh. The stinging spurns me onward. My surroundings are indistinct, the moon offering minimal light. It gives the foliage an irradiated, nightmarish quality. My bare foot tangles with a sprawling root and I stumble, the ground rushing up to meet me.

Oomph. The air jettisons out of my lungs and I languish on the forest floor, dazed. The cloying odor of upturned earth and rotting mushrooms fills my sinuses. It reminds me of death, a carcass rotting on the side of the road. My stomach churns.

With a groan, I regain my footing. My knee grinds in its socket. I think I'm bleeding. I can feel rivulets of warm fluid trickling down my shins. She'll undoubtedly be able to track me now. An errant droplet in the grass will be just as apparent to her as a trailhead. This way!

I break into a shaky, lopsided lollop. The pain threatens to usurp me, but I push it back into the very recesses of my hindbrain. I can't lose consciousness. To distract myself, I count my footfalls: one, two, one, two, one—

It helps, somewhat. Still, gray motes bob around the edges of my vision. The quick staccato of my heartbeat overtakes all other sound. My chest is on fire, my lungs trapped in an ever-tightening vice.

I can't run anymore.

Instead, I shuffle, arms outstretched, palms brushing against the scaly bark of nearby trees. The further into the forest I push, the less I can see. The moon's diffused light cannot penetrate the thickening canopy above.

In the dark, I perceive everything as both benign and nefarious. Is that a fern, or a jagged row of teeth? Is that a footfall I hear, or just an acorn loosed from its mooring overhead? Is that—

Then, I hear her growl. It's unmistakable. The sound reverberates through me, making my fingers and toes tingle. A large, slate-colored wolf-creature emerges from the shadows. She pulls her gums away from her teeth, tendrils of saliva clinging to her incisors.

"No," I breathe. Standing on her powerful hind legs, she looms head and shoulders above me.

"Found you," the wolf chortles, positively gleeful. In her almond-shaped eyes, I can see my reflection: naked, shaking, bloody. I look away, worried that I will become trapped in their amber depths, fossilized therein like a fly.

"Stay away from me," I scream, looking for some-thing—anything—to use as a weapon.

But the wolf isn't listening. She leaps atop me, knocking me flat on my back. The ground is cold, sapping all the heat from my body. Sandwiched between her huge, sinewy body and the forest floor, I feel as though I can't take a proper breath.

I push against her furred chest with my hands, but she is immovable.

My hands grow uncomfortably hot and tingly. Somehow, they have slipped inside of the wolf's pelt and the flesh underneath. It's as though she's thixo-tropic; solid unless pressure is applied like quicksand. I'm being consumed via osmosis. I kick at her, but my feet become mired, too. With a horrific sucking sound, my forearms are wrenched inside, too. No! The wolf presses her forehead against mine, and the tingling spreads across my face.

Housed inside her wolven flesh, an overpowering hunger course through me. It is so intense that it reads as nausea, as a knife sliding through my bowels.

I am aware, then, that we are not alone in the forest.

A deer watches us, her ears pricked forward. Trapped inside the wolf, I can only scream as the wolf pounces at the defenseless herbivore, sinking her teeth into its meaty haunch. I can taste the blood on my tongue, metallic and viscous, and the richness of the still-hot venison. There's an earthy, herby quality that delights the senses.

I lurch awake, kicking away the comforter. In the dark, still sleep-addled, it looks like her, me—*us*. My mouth still tastes like metal, and I gag. *It had only been a dream*, I try to reassure myself. Still, I can't shake the feeling that I had been in the forest mere moments ago. I half-expect my pajama pants to have soil stains on the knees, for leaves to adorn my hair like barrettes.

"Shit," I breathe, staring up at the ceiling. Every night is the same: a restless sleep, culminating in a gasp for air and hot tears coursing down my cheeks. The wolf doggedly pursues me through my dreams-capes, pushing aside my defenses. I press the heels of my hands into my eye sockets, letting out a short, exasperated wail. "Leave me *alone!*"

Of course, she doesn't deign to answer. She never has. She never will.

I pad down the hall to the bathroom. When I peer into the mirror, nose nearly brushing against the glass, I notice a squarish indent in my lip. I must have bitten it in my sleep. Scooping cool water from the tap, I take a long drink. The metallic taste dissipates. It's a relief. The dream felt remarkably real. Even now, I can still feel the wolf's flesh sucking me inside, con-densing me into a tight ball, stamping me down until I no longer resisted.

I can still feel the deer's life flicker between my powerful jaws.

My stomach growls.

Returning to my room, I flop down onto the rum-pled bedspread. My body feels hot, pins and needles tickling my palms and the soles of my feet. I pull my limbs close, wrapping my arms around my knees. *No, no!* The gurgling in my stomach intensifies, rolling like a storm-addled sea. *The hunger!* I can't help but think of the deer, its squarish teeth flashing as it reared away from the wolf's—*my*—snapping jaws.

The tingling creeps up my arms. In its wake, gray fur bursts from my pores. *No!* I bite my lip, hard, hoping the pain will anchor me, push the wolfish pox back within. But it doesn't work.

My ribs flare open, stretching the skin. My spine elongates with a rapid-fire *pop, pop, pop*. A bizarre pulling sensation drags my ears up to the top of my skull.

When it is over, I lay on my side, huffing. I am too big for the bed now, and the mattress sags beneath my weight. The smell of my bedspread, damp with my flop sweat, fills my nose. Then, several new scents—

I can smell them in their beds. My grandfather is asleep in the room just beside mine. I can hear the rolling thunder of his snores. I can smell the cloying peppermint of the salve he spreads on his aching joints before bed. If I concentrate hard enough, I can smell my mother's hemp eye mask and my father's woolen socks.

Beneath the artificial scent of their various creature comforts, I am aware of a tantalizing meatiness. My mouth begins to water, saliva wetting the bedspread.

I don't dare move.

CHAPTER TWO
(HALEY)

M y grandfather, Samuel Campbell, resembles a petrified pill bug. All his muscle tone has atrophied, and his flesh hangs from his deteriorating skeleton in sheets. His spine is a parenthesis, so much so, his chin rests heavily upon his sternum. Whenever I venture downstairs, he is affixed to his chair near the window, the rockers creaking on the floorboards as he seesaws back and forth, back and forth, ad infinitum.

He is well past one hundred and has been ravaged by time. In fact, he looks as though Time has grasped him in its powerful jaws and gave him a furious shake until his skin stretched. His voice is a croak, each breath a wet, sucking sound. Up close, he smells like mildew, his breath reeking of the tobacco he keeps tucked inside his cheek. I avoid him as much as I can, creeping through the front room like a wraith. I find him repugnant, but not just because of his ghoulish appearance.

"Haley," he hacks. "Can you get me some water, please?" He's spotted me, edging through the front room on my way out the door. I thought he was asleep, but every breath he takes sounds like a snore, doesn't it?

"Yeah, Papaw." I fetch a glass and fill it with cool water from the tap. When I hand it to him, he slurps it down. It flows in rivulets down his chin. I don't wipe it away like my mother does, her hands gentle. Instead, I let it moisten his collar.

"And my cigarettes," he adds, "on the end table there." He gestures with one arthritic claw at the table in question, upon which a carton of Marlboros rests.

I hesitate, eyeing the cannula coiled just beneath his nose. His oxygen tank hisses. "You aren't supposed to be smoking."

He sighs. "I'm an old man, Hale. Take pity on me."

With a sigh, I produce a cigarette, placing it gently between his chapped lips. It takes a moment to find the lighter; it's fallen on the floor, tucked just beneath the sofa. When I light it, he inhales, making the tip glow a bright red. A beacon. A warning light. Danger, danger.

"I wish you would stop looking at me like that," he mutters.

"I just did you a favor, could you not hassle me?" I groan. He is less than pleased that I detest my wolfishness. He wears his proudly. As a result of his advanced age, his wolfish attributes have burst through his human veneer. His ears are pointed, thick tufts of hair protruding from the canals. It's a wonder he can hear.

"You're ashamed," he observes. He scratches at his ear with his brittle, yellowing nails.

"I'm going out," I snap, tossing the carton of cigarettes into his lap. "Light your own cigarettes."

He dies three weeks later.

At the funeral home, I excuse myself to the bathroom. The stalls are empty, and I wash my hands. The soap smells like sandalwood and vanilla: a warm scent, reminiscent of coffee shops and smooth jazz. I scowl at my reflection: my pinched features, sallow skin, and the dark, baggy circles beneath my eyes. *I look like shit.* It looks like grief, and I don't look out of place here. But I'm not sad. *Fuck Samuel Campbell.*

My mother sat by his bedside for every torturous moment, gripping his hand in hers as he shook, gasped, asked for salvation from some God he had never spoken of before. I can't bear it.

Instead, I retreated up into the eaves of the house, sifting through the boxes in the attic. It's a silly, childish impulse—an escape wrapped in nostalgia. Sometimes, I come up here to look at the art I made as a child: portraits with stick-straight eyelashes, sketches of horses painstakingly copied from the covers of Marguerite Henry books, and little half-finished stories written about girls who talk to wolves.

I climb through the clutter and look at the boxes labeled with his name. The boxes are full of Papaw's things from before he moved in with us: clothes, mementos, bits and bobs of a long life lived. I tear the tape with my long nails and lift the flap. A puff of dust flies into the air, and I sneeze. I pull a handful of photos from the box, using the attic's dust-covered dormer window's meager light to view them.

The first is a black-and-white photograph of a man wearing a coverall, his hair slicked back. I immediately recognize the man's sharp jaw and sour expression as my grandfather. When I flip it over, I find a rolling, cursive notation: Sam, 1946.

The next photo is of a diminutive woman with dark hair, pinned tight in victory rolls. She has her arms around the young version of Papaw, both smiling so hard that their eyes crinkle. Another man, disarmingly handsome, stands behind them, his arms wrapped around them both; Sam, Rafe, and me, 1949, it says in the same curly script.

I dig through the box and produce another photo of the woman, balancing two babies on her knees. She looks up at the camera with her tongue out. The back says, in a block-print: Ama, with Jane and Cordelia.

I gaze at the infant that is my mother. Her ears are pointed, a tiny fang indenting the corner of her lip. Despite the pudgy baby cheeks and rosebud lips, perpetually pouty, I can see the adult Cordelia in her. I can see myself, too. We have been mistaken for sisters more often than I care to admit. It always makes my mom giggle and preen.

It's hot in the attic, and I rip off my beanie, tossing it aside. My hair, thick with static, stands on end. I brush my fingers through it, to no avail. Suddenly, I notice a bit of newspaper folded in half, the crease sharp. I fear that when I open it, the fragile paper will shear in half.

I open it carefully and read the article therein:

WHARTON, VIRGINIA. *A gruesome discovery was made this morning when a dead body was found by a group of beachcombers. The deceased woman was found nearly "consumed," per the Sheriff, but whether it was the cause of death is unclear.*

I pocket the article, unsure what to make of it. Why had he saved it? I carry it with me until Samuel finally stops breathing, then I tuck it under my mattress.

"Hale." My mother interrupts my reverie, her moon-like face peering into the funeral home's pristine restroom. "We have to sit down, now."

"I'll be right there," I assure her, adjusting my hair.

"Are you doing okay, honey?" she asks, opening the door a little wider. The sounds of mourners fill the room: sniffles, low voices, and the trumpet of a nose being blown.

"Yeah."

"We all miss him," Cordelia muses. "He was a good man."

I think of the article about the murdered woman under my mattress. *Was he?* She takes my arm, leading me toward the front of the viewing room. Or am I leading her? She leans into me, our hips butting together. The closer we get to the casket; the more silent tears leak out of her eyes and the more her fingers dig into my skin.

The casket is closed. But still, my mother insists we stand before it. She strokes the lid as though it's his cheek. "I'll miss you, daddy," she says.

I feel uncomfortable. I've never seen my mother so raw before, and I've certainly never stood this close to a dead body. While I can't see him, I know he's been dead just long enough to begin putrefying. It makes me feel sick, and dark motes obfuscate my vision. *Breathe, Haley,* I remind myself. But it's all for naught.

I faint.

When I come to, I'm in a side room, a matronly-looking woman sitting primly beside me. I recognize her as the funeral director. "You needn't be embarrassed, dear," she says. "It happens all the time."

"Really?" I ask as she presses a small cardboard cup into my hands. The water inside sloshes. I take a measured sip.

"Extreme emotion causes it, you know," she says earnestly.

But I don't feel emotional. Not really. There's a part of me—a deep, dark, *secret* part—that is glad Samuel Campbell is dead. He's the reason I've been saddled with this body. He's the reason my hunger never ceases.

I find myself thinking about the article, and during the reception after the service, I steal away to the attic. It's hot and humid up here; I feel as though I'm baking. I sit on the dusty floor and open a new box, finding a neatly folded military uniform. And beneath it is a book. It's leather bound, a cord tying it closed.

I unravel it, curious. Perhaps it's a first edition of some old, celebrated novel, ripe for the taking; I could make a few hundred dollars. My inheritance.

But it's not a book. It's a journal. It's written in the same block print I found before on the back of the photo of the mystery woman. *Ama*. Wasn't that her name?

September 5, 1941
I washed out. My leg still fucking hurts. Patterson pushed me off the obstacle course. Says it was an accident. Bull. Shit. Staying close—gonna try again when this heals.

Keep having bad dreams—nightmares, I guess. Starting to feel guilty. Maybe? Not really. They tasted so good. It's like having a stiffy and jerking off, having someone else jerk you off. This new town, Wharton, is full of 'em. There was this guy yesterday; he thought I was interested in him. I guess I was. But not like he thought.

He tasted like pork. God. Except—I'm now having to go out, more and more. I can't make the need go away. Not with a drink—not even with fucking.

Who wrote this? I wonder, flipping ahead, searching for a hint. Then, I find his name.

December 9, 1941
Rafe Blanchard says I can be better. I don't know what that means. But I promised to stop—for now. But god, I'm so hungry. I feel sick. I keep throwing up. I'm gonna try. I really am tired of being alone.

Mags is nice. She likes to call me Sam—not Samuel. I try to tell her I go by Samuel, but she doesn't care. She's a kidder.

But Elton...he/s a prick. He looks like a weasel and reminds me of one too. Everything he says sounds like a lie.

Sam—Samuel. This is my grandfather's journal.

They tasted so good...like pork. And he was *eating* people.

The thought sickens me. I hurriedly wrap the cord back around the book and put it back where I found it. I'll come back for it later. I don't want mom to see, not today, not while mired in her grief.

When I return to the front room, trying to smooth out the wrinkles in my dress, my father stops me. "Haley," he says "Can you help your mother in the kitchen? She's fretting over the canapés for the guests."

"Why don't you help her?" I ask, eyeing him. Clearly, he's very drunk, judging by his uncinched tie and drooping shoulders.

"C'mon, Hale. She's tired of me fawning over her. Besides, it'll keep you safe from Ms. Adams," he wheedles. Ms. Adams is our neighbor—an old biddy who talks far too much with little patience for inter-ruptions. I don't want to listen to her wax poetic about how my Papaw's death affected *her.* "She's talking to my coworker, but you know she'll set her sights on you soon," he adds.

"Fine," I snort, heading into the kitchen.

The room is bright and airy, smelling faintly of baked pastry crust and burnt sugar. My mom stands at the sink, her hands resting on the porcelain. She is looking out the window, but I recognize the far-off look; she's not here, not really.

"Mom?" I murmur, hoping not to startle her.

"Hm?" She blinks but doesn't turn toward the sound of my voice. She chews at her bottom lip, her bright red lipstick staining her teeth. It looks like blood.

"Dad said you might need help."

There are plates of nibbles on the countertop: assorted raw vegetables with hummus, ham and cheese pinwheels, and cubes of gouda stabbed with toothpicks. Flanking them are a cavalcade of lukewarm casserole dishes wrapped in cling wrap, condensed steam obscuring their contents from view.

I peel a corner back on the nearest dish, wrinkling my nose as the rank odor of tuna and cream of mushroom soup fills my sinuses.

"Can you take the plates out and pass them around?" she asks, finally meeting my eye. Cordelia is a tall, willowy woman, her ash-blond hair pulled back into a tight high ponytail. Despite her red-rimmed eyes and her smeared lipstick, she still looks lovely, otherworldly. "I put them all together, but I just can't go out there right now." Her voice wobbles.

"I've got it," I assure her. I wipe a streak of lipstick from her cheek.

With a tender smile, she cups my palm against her skin. Her fingers are cool. "Thank you, sweetheart," she murmurs. "I wish your Uncle Henry came." I'm not surprised he hadn't. My mother's brother had a human father, and made it abundantly clear he had washed his hands of the Campbell's as soon as he turned eighteen. In a way, I envied him. "We are going to miss Papaw, aren't we?" she muses, kissing my forehead.

I think of the diary entry, the way he wrote about the act of killing—the taste of long pig. He tasted like pork, he'd said.

I step away from her touch, reaching for the plates of pinwheels and veggies. "Yeah, mom," I agree half-heartedly. "Let me get these out there. Take all of the time you need."

I wait until the house is dark and quiet before I slip out of bed and creep out into the hall. Blindly, I reach up for the cord, pulling the attic stairs down. The metal whines, and I cringe. In the quiet, it sounds inordinately loud, akin to a whip crack.

Shit. I pause, listening, but there's no noise coming from my parents' room, not even the quiet rustling of the bed linen when one's sleep is disturbed.

I slowly pull the stairs down the remainder of the way and clamber up. I'm bare footed, and I am head-and-shoulders into the humid attic before I worry about stepping on an errant splinter or a tuft of loose insulation. But I don't dare go back down.

Crouching, I make my way through the attic, guiding myself by touch. Finally, near the dusty window, I find the chest, and inside, right where I'd left it…the diary. There's a part of me that wants to slam the lid closed and leave the ghosts of my grandfather's past in their graves. But I'm curious, too.

The man was a near-constant presence in my life, one I resented. But I barely knew him. Well, it's not like I really tried try to.

Once I'm safely in my room, I turn on my bed-side light. Sitting cross-legged on my bed, I open the journal, searching for another mention of murder. It doesn't take long to find it, but it's not quite in the way I expect:

[August 10, 1947]
The dead girl in the shed haunts me. I hate that she smelled so good. I hated the fear in her eyes. I hated hearing Ama scream when she stumbled upon her—the poor girl. I need to get out of Wharton. Now.

CHAPTER THREE
(CANDY)

————◁◆▷————

"Get out," I announce unceremoniously, dumping Julien's clothes onto his sleeping form.

"Hm?" Julien rolls over, his bleary eyes looking up at me. He brushes his long, auburn hair off his sloping forehead with his fingers.

For a moment, I toy with the idea of changing my mind. He's ostensibly gorgeous, and he's a particularly accommodating bedfellow. But I'm tired of him eating all of my food, sitting on my couch with his legs spread wide, and calling me "babe."

"I said 'get out,'" I reply. "We're done." The more I say it aloud, the more power the words are imbued with. I do want him to go, to disappear into the background of my life. Perhaps we will see each other on the sidewalk, incline our chins in a quiet greeting, and pass each other by. But that will be it. *Oh, he's just someone I once knew.*

"But babe—" He sits up, the blankets slipping to reveal his pert, pink nipples. "I don't understand."

"I didn't ask you to," I reply coolly. "Please, Julien, just go." He reaches for his shirt and slips it over his head before standing to pull on his boxers and jeans. His cock, thick and vascular, bobs at half-mast between his thighs. "I have a shift soon," I add, hoping to hurry him up.

But he continues to dress excruciatingly slowly.

"Can I call you later?" he asks, slipping on his shoes. "We should really talk about this. Are you on your period?"

"Out!" I snap, grasping his elbow and propelling him toward the door.

When he finally deigns to leave, I flop down onto the futon, pulling my MacBook onto my lap. My empty Google Doc is still open, the cursor blinking as if to say, *you're a failure, you're a failure, you're a failure*. I retrieve the stack of napkins off the coffee table. They are covered in sloppy pen drawings of characters, their personality traits surrounding their heads like a halo. They stare up at me—accusatory.

I sigh, the air leaving my lungs in a pronounced *woosh*. I'm not cut out to be a writer; it was a lark, little more.

As it often does when I'm meant to be writing, time hurries by. I often lose hours sitting in front of my computer, staring at my reflection in the screen. From this angle, it looks as though I have two chins, like my ski slope nose is miles long. It figures that my floundering reveals my inherent ugliness.

Stop being so hard on yourself. The words will come when they are meant to. Surely, they have to. The hours wasted on my couch can't be for naught.

I tip my phone screen and check the time. I'm already ten minutes late for my shift. Hunter will be furious.

Julien has also been texting:

[Julien: I'm sorry. what did I do wrong this time?]

I close the lid of my laptop and set it aside, stretching my long legs. Sitting cross-legged has caused them to ache, for pins and needles to travel through my toes.

Downstairs, the cafe is busy, and I hurriedly cinch my apron around my waist and step behind the counter.

My brother gives me a sharp look. "You're late," he mutters before turning on the blender. The ice inside grinds, the smell of the overheating blades faintly acrid.

"I'm sorry," I say, when he finally turns it off. "I had to kick Julien out—*again*."

Hunter raises a bushy eyebrow. "Oh yeah?" He pours cold brew over the crushed ice, topping it with a generous serving of heavy cream. "I thought you wanted to make it work."

"He was fine. I just—"

"He was a smoke show," a husky voice interrupts. Renee elbows her way between us to the cash register, her clothes smelling strongly of tar and cloves. Clearly, she has just returned from her smoke break.

"He was fine," I repeat, shrugging.

I try very hard not to entertain the secret thought: that I never found him attractive at all. Julien was hard in all the places I desired softness. His voice was too deep; his hands were too rough; his kiss was too

19

insistent. But that was the problem with all of my boy-friends, wasn't it?

Renee calls for a large mocha, and I busy myself by making it. It's late autumn, and Ebb and Flow is unseasonably busy. There's a line four people deep, and I'm grateful for it. If I'm immersed in my work, I can't think about the tumult churning inside of me.

A man—tall, muscular, dark hair flowing like a lion's mane—approaches the counter. "Are you coming?" he asks my brother, his lips pursed in a sexy pout.

"It's busy," Hunter replies. "Kiss Ama for me, Angus."

"How's she doing?" I ask, curious. I've heard rumblings that Angus' grandmother was feeling unwell. Hunter prepares lunch for her more often than not—dinner, too.

"Spends a lot of time in bed," Angus replies. I've only met her once or twice, but the thought of that vigorous woman confined to a bed seems improbable. Surely, she's frustrated by the development. "She hates that I'm doting on her," he adds with a smile.

Hunter reaches into the bakery case, then wraps a gouda and swiss sandwich in wax paper. While he slides it into a paper bag, he leans across the counter and chastely kiss Angus. "Tell her I say 'hello,'" he instructs when he pulls away.

"Absolutely," Angus replies. The paper bag crinkles in his big fist. "See you later."

"I need a flat white to go," Renee calls over her shoulder as she counts bills, sliding them into the register's open drawer.

I hurry to make it for her. First, I tip two shots of dark-colored espresso into a paper cup. Then, I froth milk, the frothing wand vibrating in my palm like an agitated hornet. Finally, I pour the milk over the espresso until the cup is full. I press the lid on.

"Flat white," I announce, my voice imbued with faux enthusiasm. It's my customer service voice.

It's nice to be busy. I make drinks, take orders, shuffle into the back room to retrieve trays of fresh pastries from Emmanuel. I nearly forget about Julien and my aborted attempt at writing as I work, focusing instead of making small talk with customers. *Where are you visiting from? Vermont? Wow, it must be so chilly there! Do I have any restaurant suggestions? Of course, try The Tailgate on Jefferson Court, their artichoke dip is to die for! Don't forget to visit our museum; it's small but we have a big history. Welcome to Wharton, welcome to Wharton, welcome to—*

Finally, we turn off the overhead lights and flip the cafe's placard from OPEN to CLOSED. My body aches; my shoulders feel inordinately tight, as if being viciously wrenched upward by an invisible force. I roll them, bending at the waist to touch my toes. My vertebrae pops.

"Have any plans tonight?" Hunter asks, wiping down the countertop in large, sweeping circles.

"No," I reply. "Not tonight."

"Do you want to get dinner with me and Angus?" he asks. It's a pity invite. He knows I'm alone now that Julien has been exiled from my loft.

"I've got to write," I reply, smoothly, though I know I'll do anything but that. "I'll see you tomorrow."

With a wave, I head into the back room, opening the door to the reeking stairwell, and above it, my loft apartment. My footfalls echo in the small, enclosed space. I climb slowly, suddenly aware of a deep pain in my thighs, courtesy of the hours on my feet.

Inside my darkened apartment, I trip over a pair of boots. They are Julien's steel-toed work boots, which he has left behind. I hate the thought of having to interact with him to return them; it'll be far too easy to slip back into his arms, into his bed. I prowl through the apartment, searching for any more remnants of him. I find a toothbrush in the bathroom, its bristles worn, but nothing else. I place it, bristles down, inside one of the boots. Hopefully, he will see it for what it is: a fuck you. *Yeah, Julien, maybe I am on my period.*

I'm too tired to write. Instead, I undress, slipping beneath the cool covers of my bedspread. Gooseflesh prickles my skin. My nipples tighten as they brush against the blankets. I'm tired, but I can't help but run my thumbs over the nubs, causing a tiny, warm ripple of pleasure to course down my body.

As I slip my hands down my taut stomach, I close my eyes, thinking of some faceless man, his abs rippling and his skin shiny with sweat. I touch myself with firm hands, knowing how best to reach orgasm. But try as I might, as vigorously as I stroke with shaking fingers, I can't reach that moment of release. Instead, I waver on the cliff edge.

It's okay to think about it, I tell myself. *No one will know.*

I wrinkle my brow, pressing my lips tightly together. *No one will know.* I press a finger inside my warmth, stroking the textured walls therein. The fantasy man fades away, and I turn my attention to a new, salacious reverie: a fantasy woman.

CHAPTER FOUR
(HALEY)

———◁◆▷———

I have always had dreams of running. We all do: bounding through brush, kicking up clods of dirt, chasing the white tails of frightened prey. In mine, I run fast, leaping over downed trees, my bare feet slapping against the bark. I fjord streams, the icy cold water turning my toes blue and numb. I climb hills, hand over foot, huffing.

I dread the dreams. I hate the moment when I inevitably corner my prey, when the wolfishness in me bursts forth.

I stand in the doorway as my mother prepares to hunt, stripping naked in the backyard. "Won't you come?" she asks.

I press my lips together, nostrils flaring. "No," I reply shortly. I wish she would stop asking.

My father, sitting at the kitchen table, offers me a small smile. He's staying in tonight, having tweaked his ankle the night before. "We can play a board game," he suggests. "How about you beat your old man at Monopoly?"

But I ignore him, instead watching as my mother transforms. Silvery fur trickles down her back, spreading across her buttocks. Her hipbone dislocates and tips violently to one side, the right ilium nearly bursting through her thin skin. She falls heavily onto her left side, her hand starfished on the moist earth. I rush across the wet grass to help her, pulling her back to her feet. She's heavier now, and the exertion makes sweat prickle on my brow.

She turns her long, tapered snout in my direction, a huff of hot air rushing across my cheek. "You're sure?" she asks in her now-grumbly voice.

"Yeah, I'm sure," I reply. "Be safe, mom." I pat her furred shoulder and head back to the house. When I glance back, she is gone, the leaves rustling in her wake. She knows better than to push, to cajole.

"Are you sure you don't want to play?" my father asks, gesturing to the pile of board games tucked beneath the china hutch: Monopoly, Parcheesi, Mancala, Life, and Trouble. Mancala used to be my favorite. I liked to hold the smooth stones in my hand, their coolness sapping the heat from my palm.

"Yeah. I'm going upstairs."

It's still so strange to be in my childhood bedroom. The vallances are a bright pink, and the wallpaper border is a cheerful polka dot. The corkboard is still covered in drawings of horses I did as a teen, the corners curling and yellowed with age. The entirety of my adult life is in boxes stacked in the closet, placed haphazardly around the room. One, filled with clothing, is open, clothes spilling down the side like an avalanche.

"Get the fuck out," Gina snaps, shoving a handful of my clothes into my arms. "I'm tired of picking up the slack while you sit on your ass with your stupid headphones on."

"Gee," I manage. Her accusation isn't entirely unfounded. I have been spending the majority of my time on the couch becoming mired there in a nest of empty potato chip bags, unfinished job applications, and blankets that become smellier with each passing day.

"Don't 'Gee' me," she interrupts. "You know, I've let a lot of shit go. But you're three months behind on your half of the rent. I'm not your mother, and I refuse to act like it." She runs her hands through her thick, glossy hair. "I'm done, Haley."

I reach for her hand, squeezing her fingers. "I'm looking for a job, I swear. Give me one more month." I tug on her hand, pulling her close, caressing her cheek. "Come on," I wheedle, looking into her grey eyes.

Despite herself, she leans into my touch, heaving a sigh. "I love you, Hale," she murmurs. "I really do."

"I can do better," I promise as I tug at the buttons of her blazer, loosening one, then another. "I'll call around tomorrow." I don't tell her I have no one to call. I've run out of favors, leads, all of it. I've burnt most of my bridges. I haven't been able to keep a job for more than a month or two, and my friendships seem to disintegrate just as quickly.

Methodically, I slip her blazer off her shoulders, letting it fall to the carpet. It will wrinkle, and she'll inevitably be upset about it, but right now, her eyes are half-lidded, and her breath is quickening. That's it. *But, when I begin to work on the buttons of her blouse, her jaw tightens into a sharp angle.*

"You're not listening to me," she grumbles, roughly pushing my hands away.

"I hear you," I assure her.

"No," she snaps. "You don't." Gina grabs her blazer off the floor and smooths it over her arm. Before slamming the bedroom door in my face, she puts the final nail in my coffin: "I want you out by Sunday."
Sunday—our one-year anniversary

Or rather, what would have been our one-year anniversary.

I flop belly-first onto my bed, reaching beneath the mattress for my grandfather's journal. The pages reek of rancid wood pulp, and I wrinkle my nose. I've never liked the smell of old books. It makes my skin feel greasy, like each turn of the page coats my fingers in antiquity. Soon, I think, my scent will be indistinguishable from that of a mummified cat trapped in the walls.

I open the book to the first page:

[May 31, 1941]
I need to leave Ridgerton. The cops are starting to notice the bodies piling up. I'm heading to Virginia in a few weeks for Basic. I just can't hunt 'til then. God, how am I supposed to go back to deer? Even my mother's home cooking doesn't compare.

[June 8, 1941]

I fucked up. Shit. Marnie just looked so pretty in that dress, and she smelled so good. I took her out on the town: ate at the Dairy Queen, saw that new movie The Maltese Falcon, *then went up to the reservoir for some peace and quiet. She was eager—god, so eager— but her skin was salty with sweat. I meant to just have a little lick...*

I dumped her in the reservoir. Maybe they won't ever find her.

The journal entries are both nauseating and gripping. It's akin to rubbernecking at an accident site: not wanting to see the carnage but unable to tear one's eyes away. I always considered the impulse as a need to bear witness, to acknowledge someone's very worst day. Is that what I'm doing here? Or is this something else altogether?

I close the journal, tucking it back into its hiding space. I can almost feel it thrumming—my very own telltale heart. I long to throw it away, to cast it aside, but I feel tethered to it.

I need to get out of the house.

Ridgerton is a small city just outside of Knoxville. No one ever says they are from Ridgerton. It was once a thriving city, but most of its charm had been mowed over, replaced by apartment complexes and suburbs within suburbs. The only place open this late is the Exxon, with its one perpetually flickering bulb beneath the canopy and the bored-looking teenaged cashier behind the register. I stop for gas, filling the tank just enough to get by.

I drive into Knoxville in my beat up Rav4, parking in the cement garage off Market Square. It's nearly 11:00 p.m., but the downtown walking mall is crowded; it's Friday after all. I wind my way through drunk revelers — most of which are young adults sporting University of Tennessee merchandise.

The mouth-watering tang of Soccer Taco — a bouquet of cilantro, carne asada, tortilla chips flash-fried in piping hot oil — entices me inside the small Mexican restaurant. I sit at the bar, self-consciously pulling my beanie down over my ears. I haven't been in public in a long time. I've been the ghost haunting my parent's house, the one they thought they had exorcised.

"What can I get you?" the bartender asks. She's pretty, with a short gingery bob and a smattering of freckles across her nose. A septum ring dangles between her nostrils, catching the light.

"Can I get a Modelo and a taco salad?" I ask, knowing my order by heart.

Gina and I used to be regulars here. In fact, we used to live in an apartment complex just two blocks away. She may still live there; we haven't spoken in months, not since I moved out. As I often do, I find myself wanting to call her. I've almost hit DIAL countless times over the last several weeks, wanting — *needing* — someone else to bear witness to the journal's loathsome contents.

"Sure thing," the bartender replies. She grabs a chilly bottle of Modelo, popping the top with a practiced flick of the bottle opener. "Here you go, doll," she says, giving me a wink. She's wearing glittery eyeshadow. I can feel a hot blush creeping up my neck.

"Thanks." I take a sip, wiping a dribble off my chin.

While the bartender moves onto other customers, she keeps glancing in my direction, her teeth coyly indenting the corner of her lip. I cross my legs, suddenly aware of a deep ache in my groin. It's been such a long time since I've been with someone, touched someone, been touched. God.

When my salad arrives, she slides it across the bartop. "Enjoy," she says. The salad is enormous, housed within a fried tortilla bowl. Inside, leafy green lettuce is adorned with refried beans, tomato, shredded beef, and a hefty dollop of sour cream.

I scoop a bit of lettuce and bean into my mouth, chewing slowly. "Thanks," I manage mid-swallow. The bartender rests her palms on the bartop, leaning forward just enough for me to catch a glimpse of the creamy skin beneath her V-neck. The freckles dot her chest too—tiny constellations.

"Y'know," she says, the words coming as slow as molasses. "I get off in an hour, if you're interested." She tucks a strand of hair behind her ear, revealing enormous opal plugs and a veritable latticework of stainless steel decorating her cartilage. She reminds me of Gina, who stretched her lobes and had a tiny heart tattoo just behind her ear. When she wore clear plugs, I could see the tattoo through the glass, the edges warped.

I stare dumbly at her. It's not that I don't understand what she's insinuating, I *do*. It's her apparent interest that floors me. Gina would often tell me how beautiful I was, but I didn't believe her. Not really. How could someone be beautiful with these impulses? Surely, it has stained me.

I tug at my beanie.

Her face blanches, she's taken my silence as offense. "I'm *so* sorry, forget I've said anything. Look...your meal is on me, okay? I'm sorry, I—" Her hands flap, as if she can shoo the invitation away.

"I'm very interested," I assure her. "I'm just horrifically out of practice interacting with other human beings." I grin. "I'm Haley." I offer her my hand to shake, and she cups it between both of hers warmly.

"Tara," she says, the corner of her lip twitching into a tentative smile. "Maybe we could go across the street and have a drink?" she suggests.

"I'd like that."

While I finish my dinner, I covertly watch Tara work. She is everything I am not: boisterous, loud, seemingly confident in her skin. From time to time, she flashes me a smile as if to say, *I haven't forgotten about you*. It's as though she can sense my trepidation. I am excited to spend time with her, but I can see it for what it is, what it will be: fleeting. She'll see me for what I am and run screaming.

Tara brings me the bill, sliding it across the bartop as if we are engaging in an illicit transaction. "I have to clock out," she says, "I'll be back in a few minutes."

While I wait, I pick at the hem of my sweater. It's old and shabby, loose strings protruding from between the zig-zag stitching. I tug on one, loosing another, ad infinitum. If I am left to my own devices for too much longer, I fear that it will only be tatters.

"I'm back," Tara announces from behind me, her palm resting on my shoulder. "Are you ready?"

"Yeah," I reply. "Let's go."

The bar across the street is called Culvers. It's a tight space, consisting of the bar proper and a rooftop lounge. I've been here once or twice. I have a hazy memory of puking in the bathroom, Gina stroking my hair. It's packed, and Tara and I have to hold hands to avoid being separated in the crowd. Tara leads the way, cutting through the crowd like a hot knife in butter.

She knows the bartender, and she is able to bypass the queue of waiting patrons to get us a couple of beers. "Is a stout okay?" Tara asks, leaning close so I can hear her over the din. I nod my assent. The crowd—itself an amorphous thing—pushes us together, hip to hip. I am suddenly very aware of my body, how my body fits with her body. My breath catches.

"Let's go upstairs," she urges when the beers arrive. I follow her up the staircase, trying very hard not to spill my beer nor look at her ample ass.

A cool breeze ruffles my hair. It's a relief to be outdoors. While the rooftop is equally as crowded as downstairs, it is far less claustrophobic. I no longer feel as though I'm breathing the same hot air as hundreds of other patrons. I had nearly convinced myself I was suffocating. Or was that the result of feeling Tara so close? Maybe I was drowning in her.

I would like to.

Tara and I find a small, unoccupied cafe table. It is so tiny we are nearly sitting atop each other—her knee between my thighs and mine between hers. She takes a swig of her beer, looking at me through her eyelashes.

"What?" I ask, that same blush blooming on my chest, up my neck, cupping my cheeks in its rosy glow.

"I remember you, you know," she replies, picking at the edges of her bottle's label. "You used to come into the restaurant a lot with that girl."

"I didn't realize I was so memorable," I reply, trying very hard not to think about Gina.

"How could I forget the hat?" Tara reaches across the table, plucking at the hem of my beanie. Her fingertips are cool on my forehead. "I had a huge crush on you, but you were clearly unavailable."

"*Me?*" Gina was always the one who batted off admirers. Both men and women often stared at her and looked at me with something akin to astonishment. *How did* she *snag* her? I was—am—a tomboyish woman with a preference for boxy tees, skinny jeans, and high-tops. Conversely, Gina dressed as though she had a runway to walk, heads to turn. She was imbued with a preternatural confidence, cognizant of her desires and expecting nothing less. An alpha wolf.

"I know what I like," Tara says with a shrug. "When I saw you tonight, *alone*, I figured I would shoot my shot."

I gulp my beer, looking for confidence in its dark depths. "I'm glad you did," I finally say. Tara's thigh presses against mine. It's intentional, firm. I touch her knee beneath the table, tracing the pattern of her fishnet tights with my fingertips.

"Do you want to dance?" she asks huskily, gesturing to the small dancefloor, twinkle lights crisscrossed above it.

I don't, but I do want to touch her. I nod.

Tara rises, reaching for my hand. I take it, swallowing the remainder of my beer. When we step into the midst of dancing bodies, she turns and faces me, pulling me close. I rest my hands on her hips. The music — some dance track, inconsequential — thrums beneath our feet, imbuing us with a frenetic energy. My heart beats in tempo, spurred on by Tara's hands slipping beneath my sweater.

I press my face into the curve of her neck. She smells so much different than my former girlfriend, who always smelled earthy — *wild*. Tara smells like perfume, but there's something else, too —

He tasted like pork. Her skin was salty with sweat. That's what he had written, wasn't it?

Saliva pools in my mouth. I can't discern if it's from hunger or needing to vomit, and that terrifies me. Gooseflesh prickles my skin. But Tara is entirely unaware. Her groin presses against mine, causing tiny sparks of pleasure to zing through my core. I press my lips against the tissue paper thin skin of her neck.

The track changes, the tempo a slow roll. Tara's arms encircle my neck, and she kisses my mouth. Her tongue tastes like beer. I am unprepared for the urge to bite it off. I want to tell her to stop, I want to tell her I have to go home. But I'm just *so hungry* for her, in every conceivable way.

"Let's go somewhere more private," I find myself saying.

"My apartment," she breathes. "It's just one street over."

Tara's apartment is a small studio. We barely make it through the door before I start stripping her of her clothes. First, I pull her tee over her head, pulling down the cups of her bra. She mewls when I take her nipple into my mouth, gently sucking it into an aching point. Her skin is pink with desire, blotchy with my kisses.

Tara peels off my sweater, slipping her hands inside my button-down shirt. "God, you're so hot," she exclaims as she fumbles with the buttons.

I'm practically panting as I pull the zipper on her skirt, tossing the rectangle of fabric aside. I kiss down her abdomen, falling to my knees between her legs. When I lick her thigh through her tights, my stomach clenches tight. I want to sink my teeth into the fatty flesh there so, so badly.

No, Haley. This isn't you. You're drunk and confused.

My gums itch, my teeth crowding my mouth. I tear at Tara's tights. Tara groans, pressing her hips toward my face, my mouth. She pulls my beanie off, making my hair frizzy and stand on-end. "Wait," she murmurs, pushing my hair back, her fingertips touching the growing point of my ear.

But then, she's screaming, and hot blood fills my mouth.

CHAPTER FIVE
(CANDY)

———◁◆▷———

I tip my chair back, chewing at my pen cap. My professor drones on about Proust, but I'm not entirely listening. Out the window, I can see the campus courtyard, and just beyond it, the tiniest sliver of beach. The sun is nearly touching the horizon, paint strokes of pink and purple demarcating daylight from dusk. I've been dreading this all day.

When the lecture ends, I find my car in the parking lot, wedged between an SUV and pickup. The latter is too close, and I have to suck in my stomach to squeeze by. I open the garment bag draped across the backseat, pulling out a black dress. Despite my best efforts, it's still somewhat wrinkled. But she won't mind.

Casting my eyes left and right, I remove my blouse, tossing it amidst the discarded coffee cups on the floor. I slip the dress over my head, pulling it down over my hips. I slip my sneakers and jeans off. A passerby gives me an odd look, and I raise my eyebrows. *What are you looking at?* The asphalt is hot beneath my naked feet, and I shift from foot to foot, searching for my heels. I find them beneath the front seat.

My phone buzzes, still in my jeans pocket.

[Hunter: You're late]

"I'm coming," I groan. I would like to drive in the opposite direction. But instead, I head toward the agreed upon location: a small inlet on the south-side of Wharton. It's a quiet place, the foliage over-head keeping it cool, even in the dead of summer. It used to be my mother's favorite place. She called it Tranquil Cove.

I park a half mile away, the bollards delineating the road from the trail keeping me from driving any further. Hunter's car is already here, the engine ticking at it cools. If I hurry, I might be able to catch up with them on the trail.

An ancient Toyota pickup rumbles up the road, parking next to my Volkswagen. The driver flicks a cigarette butt out the window before easing out, his movements slow and deliberate. "Come help your old man, Candy," he grumbles, hacking a globule of spit onto the dirt.

"Hey, daddy," I reply, taking his elbow. I haven't seen him since Christmas. It's as though he has aged a decade in the months since then. His hair is more salt than pepper. His crow's feet are veritable cavities, revealing the layers of lives lived. The skin on his fore-head and cheeks is blotchy with keratosis, an aftereffect of a lifetime of sun exposure and poor skincare.

We walk together past the bollards, our shoes crunching on gravel. I immediately regret wearing heels. It'll be a wonder if I don't sprain my ankle.

"How's school?" he asks, not attempting to conceal the derision in his voice.

I wince. "It's fine," I reply shortly.

He thinks getting an MFA is a waste of time, little more than a silly whim. If he had his way, I would be in business school, following in my brother's footsteps. Hunter is, after all, a pillar of the community—someone to be proud of. I'm the freeloader, while Hunter owns the building in which I live and pays my salary.

We walk in silence, listening to the birds chatter. The foliage thickens, the branches interwoven overhead. Sunlight dapples the path ahead. The sounds of the ocean grow louder. We're nearly there.

My father sighs. "Candy," he says. "I'm just worried about you, is all."

"I didn't ask you to be," I reply.

"Your mom—"

"Can we not do this today?" I beg, cutting him off. "Please. Just give it a rest for one evening." Hot, angry tears well up in my eyes, and I swipe them away with the heel of my hand. I feel flayed open, each nerve ending firing off the same dispatch: *pain, pain, pain.*

I don't want to be here. I want to go home and crawl into my bed.

Finally, we step out onto the thin strip of beach. Hunter waves. He's wearing his only suit: a dark gray Kenneth Cole with the buttons undone. It's the same suit he wore to the funeral years ago when he was much smaller, but now, the fitting is poor. When he raises his arm, I can see his entire wrist.

Angus stands next to his boyfriend. He's more groomed than I am accustomed to: his beard has been trimmed; his hair is pulled back into a tight, moussed ponytail; and he's wearing a black Jos. A. Bank suit. Somehow, it makes him appear even broader than he is, the buttons tugging at the buttonholes.

"Let's get started," I say without preamble. I open the cooler Hunter brought along, pulling out a bouquet of chrysanthemums, snapdragons, and puffs of cremone. The majority of the flowers are yellow with pops of white here and there. Mom would have liked it very much. I drape it over my forearm, the spray of snapdragons tickling my ribs through my thin dress.

Hunter raises his eyebrows at me, as if to say, *are you okay?*

I just shake my head, clutching the bouquet tight. It's a relief to hold something, to have something to do with my hands.

"Thirteen years ago, today," Hunter begins, his words practiced, "we lost this family's foundation. This is always a sad day—guttingly so—but it's also a good one because we get to talk about mom."

I don't want to talk about mom.

"I was twenty when she died," Hunter continues, "and I had just bought the cafe. She would come visit sometimes after chemo. I think she knew I was in over my head, and she would spend hours asking me question after question. And it wasn't because she didn't know the answers—she absolutely did! She asked so I would take a deep breath and think it through. She knew…"

He pauses, scuffing his shoe in the sand. His Adam's apple bobs as he tries not to cry. "She knew she wouldn't be here for very long. She wanted to become that voice inside my head, the one that asked, 'what about, what if?' And it's funny, because sometimes, when I'm balancing the books, I'll hear, 'Hunter, why are you paying so much for artisanal cream cheese?'" He chuckles, the sound devoid of humor.

"I love you, mom," he finishes. "I miss you. I wish—I wish that you could see how your kids are doing, you would be so proud."

Beside me, my father coughs.

Would she be proud? Hunter's eyes meet mine. He wants me to say something. But what can I possibly say, and who would it benefit? My grief feels so personal now: a fragile little Fabergé egg I keep tucked away for safekeeping. It's not a spectacle. It's not for my dad or brother to gawk at, to poke.

"I love you, mom," I finally say, burying my nose in the puffy chrysanthemums and inhaling their herby scent. Mom liked them because they looked pretty but weren't particularly fragrant. *Smelling nice isn't the point*, she'd said, *it's a message to the insects: fuck off!* "See you next year," I add as an afterthought. It's pithy and a bit sardonic, but I don't think mom would have minded. I kneel, placing the bouquet in the water. The water laps against the cellophane as I untie it, letting the flowers drift away. They fan out into a great arc, carried out into the sea.

"You were supposed to wait until the end," Hunter huffs.

I ignore his outburst. Dad is speaking now, his voice a low grumble reverberating through me. But, I don't listen to his elegy. Instead, I watch the flowers until it gets too dark to see.

CHAPTER SIX
(HALEY)

———◁◆▷———

I wake with a gasp. I'm in an unfamiliar place, the sun pouring in through the half-closed blinds. I sit up, my head swimming. I'm thirsty; my tongue feels too large for my mouth, grainy like sandpaper. I'm still in the same clothes I wore the night before, but they're rumpled, stiff with an unknown substance. Did I spill something?

I must have had more to drink than I thought.

I only remember bits and pieces of the night before: dancing with Tara at the rooftop bar, kissing her on the street outside of her apartment building, and undressing her in the dark. This must be her apartment.

I stumble to the kitchenette, fishing an ice cube out of the freezer. I pop it into my mouth, the cool liquid trickling down the back of my tongue. "Tara?" I say aloud. *Where is she?*

My head pounds, the pain radiating with every heartbeat. I head back to the futon, intending to flop back down onto the thin mattress. But then, I see a pile of blankets on the floor, and peeking out from beneath them, Tara's hand. She's wearing coral-colored nail polish, the tips filed into blunt almonds.

"Tara?" I call hesitantly. I feel like I'm walking through molasses. Suddenly, I smell it: cloying, coppery. The metallic odor fills my nostrils, trickling down my sinuses into the back of my throat. I heave. "Tara?" I whimper, reaching toward the blankets with a trembling hand. *She's just sleeping,* I soothe myself, *we drank too much, and she passed out.*

"Wait," Tara's voice is like a lance, the point slicing into my shoulder, knocking me off-balance. I look up at her. Her mouth is slack, her brows knitted. "Wait," she repeats, breathy. Her thumb strokes the furred slope of my ear, palpating as if looking for a seam. She thinks it's a costume. She can't even contend with the thought that my ears are genuine. That would be crazy, *and Tara isn't a crazy girl.*

I should stop, say something to placate her, and go home. But all I can smell is her salty skin, and I'm so hungry. It's as though I haven't eaten in a thousand years. My dinner may as well have been bowl of sawdust, tasteless, bland. I press a soft kiss on her thigh and inhale.

My teeth itch. Just one taste, *a little voice whispers into my ear.* Just one, just one, just one.

I tug on the corner of the blanket, revealing her shoulder and the delicate slope of her clavicle, inch by inch. She doesn't move, nor murmur. *She's dead.* The thought becomes a wave and crashes against my chest, causing me to stumble backward. The blanket, knotted in my fist, shears away from her supine form. Tara is nearly naked, save for her underwear and tights, arms and legs akimbo. Her leg is mangled, swaths of meat missing as if it had been scooped out.

I can't stay here.

"I'm so sorry," I mumble. "I'm so, so sorry." But then, I see it: a strand of hair, draped across her lips, fluttering. She's breathing. I scrabble for her purse, searching for her phone. I toss aside lipstick, tampons, and a small bottle of hand sanitizer before I find it. With shaking hands, I swipe to the emergency screen, squinting when the blinding white light lances through my sensitive retinas, and tap 9-1-1.

"9-1-1, what is your emergency?" a tinny voice asks.

"My friend," I manage. My tongue feels dry and thick, sticking to the roof of my mouth, muffling my words. "She's dying."

"Your friend is dying?" A racket of typing punctuates the question.

"She's bleeding. She's barely breathing." I'm pacing, coursing up and down the living room in long strides. I try very hard not to look at Tara's supine form, the pool of blood creating a halo around her. I can hear her breathing now; it's a grinding, crackling sound deep in her lungs, leaking from her parted lips. I rattle off the address, or as close to it as I can manage. "Apartment 3B, the front door is open."

Before the dispatcher can ask anything else, I set the phone on the arm of the couch. I burst from the apartment, gulping the fresh air. I nearly tumble down the stairs, streaking across the street toward the parking garage. I am grateful for the early hour. The street—the sidewalk—is nearly empty.

A man walking his Bichon passes by on the opposite side of the street, but he doesn't give me a second glance.

When I finally lock myself inside the car, I grind my fists into my eye sockets. Starbursts crowd my vision, and I blink them away. Despite no longer being in the apartment, I can still smell iron. Then, I realize my clothes are covered in her coagulating blood; my tee is inelastic, laying oddly on my frame. Sobbing, my body heaving, I pull out onto the street. But I don't take the exit back to Ridgerton.

Instead, I ease onto I-81.

I'm not sure what I expected of Wharton. Samuel Campbell had written so little about the town itself, but it is small, wedged between unincorporated woodland and the Atlantic Ocean. When I crack the window open, the sea air rushes in—briny and balmy. My body aches; I drove for five hours non-stop, and I'm desperate for a stretch and a pee. It doesn't take long before I find a hotel on the main strip, called the Wharton Great Inn.

I adjust the rearview mirror and survey my reflection. I look road-weary: my skin blotchy and my hair a rat's nest. I tease out the knots with my fingers, braiding the length into a single plait. My beanie—stinking of dried sweat—covers the frizz. It's hot, but I grab my olive-green jacket from the backseat. I can't check in with bloody clothes; zipped up, the jacket hides the worst of it.

I trot inside the hotel, bag in hand. It's September, but sweat prickles on my forehead, soaking the folded brim of my hat. The lobby is rife with tourists, many of whom are crowded around a small buffet table. I can smell bacon. My stomach clenches. I can't seem to get the taste of blood from my mouth. I chewed an entire pack of wintergreen gum during the trip, but it just made me feel queasy.

I'm not sure why I'm here. At first, I just couldn't bear the thought of going home. Then, I started thinking about my grandfather's pilgrimage here. He stopped writing about the hunger, the bloodshed, after washing out in Wharton. *Rafe says I can be better.* Maybe he can help me, too, assuming he is still alive. He may not even live here anymore.

The bored-looking man at the front desk barely glances up as I approach. "Can I help you?" he asks in a slow, rolling drawl.

"I need a room for a week," I reply. "Single bed."

"Do you have a reservation?" He smells of after-shave, an artificial earthiness. It fills my nostrils, deadening my senses. It's a relief; I don't want to smell him. I don't want to feel that hunger again.

"Do I need one?" I ask meekly.

"Well," he huffs, "if you want a room *here* then yes, you do. We simply don't have any rooms left. Not even a coat closet."

"Are there any other hotels nearby?" My voice sounds two octaves too high. I didn't think this through. I haven't had a single substantial thought in hours. I've just been operating on instinct: run, run, run, sidestep the traps.

"Keep going down Main for another three blocks. There's a motel there: the Cove. It'll have vacancies — always does." He shoos me away with a flick of the wrist, already looking past me toward the next guest.

The Cove Motel is, just as he said, three blocks down Main Street. The parking lot is nearly empty, the asphalt cracked as if slapped by an enormous hand. There's a courtyard with a pool, but the water is still, oily with algae. I stand in the courtyard for a few moments, staring up at the motel's mermaid-shaped sign. Someone had graffitied over the cursive *Cove Motel* signage with the word DUMP.

"It'll have vacancies, huh?" I mutter. Something tells me I'll be sharing a room with a whole army of bedbugs.

The front office reeks of cigarette smoke. It's humid, a small oscillating fan offering very little relief. The desk is occupied by a teenager, her chin resting heavily on her palm. She doodles with her free hand, decorating the margins of an invoice with curlicues and flowers. "Welcome to the Cove Motel," she chirps.

"Can I get a room?" I ask.

"Sure." She shrugs. "How long will you be staying with us?" She wakes her computer with a keystroke.

"A week," I reply.

"Your name?"

"Haley Campbell." I slide my credit card across the countertop. "Do you know where I can find someone called Rafe Blanchard?" I ask. It's a long shot. I might not even be pronouncing it correctly.

47

"Can't say that I do," the girl answers, typing. She hands me a keycard. "Welcome to Wharton. You're in Room Six." I've been dismissed.

I find the room with no trouble, tapping the keycard against the sensor. It unlocks with a hollow *thwunk*. The room is small, made up of a king-sized bed, a squat refrigerator, a dresser with a television perched on top, and a humming air conditioner. I drop my purse on the bed and head into the attached bathroom. The shower is mildewy, but in my eyes, it's an oasis. I desperately want to wash the events of the night before off me, scrubbing until my skin sloughs off and I am born anew.

Stepping under the hot spray, I scrub my scalp with my nails. As I squirt a dollop of shampoo into my palm, I start to cry. *Tara. Oh god, what have I done?* Sobs ratchet me in half, and I slap my palm against the linoleum to keep from toppling over. I can still taste her in my mouth, feel her phantom flesh split as I sink my serrated teeth into her thigh. I can't remember what happened after that first bite, and that makes me feel worse. Did Tara suffer? Did the blood loss teleport her elsewhere, to some cotton-wrapped part of her consciousness where pain no longer exists?

I stay in the shower until the water runs cool. After, I slip into the same, dingy outfit. The crusty fabric rubs painfully against my skin, made sensitive by the heat. *I need new clothes.*

CHAPTER SEVEN
(LEIGH)

---◁◆▷---

I take a detour just south of Wharton, parking my rental car just off West Road in Chesapeake. It's early in the evening, and the near-constant humidity has abated somewhat; the trailhead is clogged with pedestrians. A bicyclist whizzes past me, so close the backdraft lashes my hair against my neck. I scowl at his retreating back, the Rorschach blot of sweat adorning his fluorescent cycling jersey.

I walk a half-mile before easing off the paved trail, heading into the wetlands. It seems familiar enough: I walk along a game trail, trampling long stalks of grass and tripping over tree roots. In only a few minutes, the toes of my sneakers sink into the swampy shore of the Great Dismal Swamp. The water is still, the branches of the overhanging cypress trees reflected therein. I'm not entirely sure if this is the right spot, but it's close enough.

"Hey, James," I say to the still water. A heron, nearby, thrusts its head into the water, then comes up for air with a perch gripped in its beak. I watch it gulp it down, the lump of bone and meat slowly easing down its narrow esophagus. I can't help but to imagine what swallowing bone would feel like—sharp, unyielding.

I sit on the bank, taking off my shoes and socks. I want to put my feet into the murky water. James is in here somewhere, and I want to feel close to him. The water is chilly, and I wiggle my toes when they become tingly. Pressing my heels into the mud, I giggle when the earth slurps against my skin. Out here, I feel strangely giddy, manic.

Wolfish, I wade out into the water, stopping only when it laps against my breastbone. James, in my arms, is nearly submerged, save for his face. In the dark water, I can vaguely see the shadow of his limbs, his arms outstretched as if seeking supplication. Death has smoothed his features, making him appear younger than his thirty-three years. For the thousandth time, I try to close his eyes, but they remain half-lidded. It feels as though he's glaring at me.

I disappointed him. Perhaps if I fought harder, he would have had the upper hand. He should have; it was three against one, wasn't it? But my heart wasn't in it, not really. I didn't want to hurt Angus. Though, I also didn't think Angus would ever hurt James.

I am haunted by the sound of James' vertebrae grinding together, Angus' grunt of exertion. Angus' eyes were closed as he crushed my twin's windpipe, shattered the cervical spine. I suspect he couldn't bear to see it. But I saw the light snuff from James' eyes. I had thought that was a euphemism, a poetic way to describe the moment when the soul is torn from the flesh. Light's out—no one's home. Except, it truly happened; his pupils usurped his irises, the sclera lost its luster.

"I'm sorry," I whisper, loosening my grip. James' body sinks below the water. When he finally reaches the swamp floor, the sediment whirls up around him, obscuring him from view. It's as though he's been swallowed, digested.

I don't know why I do it. With a strangled sob, I dive down beneath the water, reaching for him. The water stings my eyes. I can't let him go. I want to hold him again, cradle him against my furred chest like a slumbering infant. At least, when he was close, I could pretend I was whole. The moment he fell from my arms, it was as though I was a forest that had been burnt; nothing remained but char and ash. I could almost taste it on my tongue. If I swallowed, I feared I would choke.

Luka splashes into the water behind me, wrapping his muscular arms around my midsection as he hauls me up. "Leigh!" he shouts, his wolven voice glottal. "Stop it, stop! He's gone!"

I elbow my pack mate in the snout, diving again. My claws briefly touch what I think is James' cheek before Luka drags me to the surface again.

He holds me tight, pinning my arms. "He's gone," he murmurs into my ear, "he's gone."

I linger on the bank of the swamp until the sun goes down. The cypress trees—their flared roots emerging from the mire like hulking Titans—groan as the breeze rustles their outstretched branches. The frogs begin to sing. In the distance, I hear a muted splash; something toothy has entered the water, searching for a meal. Bats swoop noisily into the foliage, catching insects. Mosquitos buzz around my ears, leaving raised welts on my skin.

He's gone, just like Luka said. But I can feel him here.

"I'm sorry," I say aloud. "I'm going to make it up to you."

"Miss?" Something taps against the half-open window next to my head, and I jerk awake. The sky is grey, sunrise encroaching on the horizon. I must have fallen asleep after walking back to my car. It had taken twice as long to backtrack in the dark, getting turned around more than once.

The man at the window shines his flashlight directly into my eyes, and I cover my face with my forearm. "Sorry," he says, aiming at my lap instead. I wish he would turn it off. "You can't sleep here, Miss." The man is wearing a short-sleeved khaki button-down and olive-colored shorts, hemmed just above the knees. An embroidered badge on the shirt breast reads U.S FISH & WILDLIFE SERVICE.

"Sorry, officer." I yawn, rolling my aching shoulders. "I'll be on my way." I reach for the car keys, nestled in the passenger seat between an empty Dasani bottle and a Wawa bag with a half-eaten sub sandwich inside. The key fob is attached to an ugly plastic key-chain with Hertz printed on it.

"It's illegal to be on federal property after posted hours. I have to write you a ticket," he says. "Could you step out of the car for a few minutes, please?"

Shit. I do as instructed, keys still in hand.

The officer places his flashlight on the hood of the car, the beam of light streaking across the deserted parking lot. It warps the shadows of a nearby pine tree, making it appear ominous. It looks like it would feel more at home outside of a haunted house.

"Can we just forget about this?" I ask. "I really didn't mean to."

The officer sighs. "I can't do that. Do you have your license and registration?"

I reach into my back pocket for my wallet and retrieve the registration from the pocket in the driver's side door. "It's a rental," I explain as I open my wallet, sliding my driver's license out of its clear sleeve. A folded photo falls out, fluttering to the asphalt. I quickly retrieve it, stuffing it back inside. I don't want to look at it. Though, I don't have to. The image there is burned into my hippocampus.

It's a photo of James, Angus, and I. James and Angus are sitting on the couch in their Portland loft, and I'm laying across their laps. I have a beer in-hand, the bottle precariously tilted, the amber liquid infringing on the lip. Angus' eyes are the size of dinner plates, and he's mid-shout ("Leigh, be *careful!*"). James, conversely, has a Cheshire Cat grin, a joint dangling from between his lips. He has one arm slung over the back of the couch, his fingertips resting on Angus' bunched shoulder. It was a happy time, before James' veneer cracked.

James lurches into my apartment, not bothering to knock.

"Excuse you!" I shout. I'm getting dressed, a pair of jeans midway up my thighs. But he doesn't seem to notice at all; he's not looking at me. "Have you ever thought about it?" he rambles, opening my fridge and helping himself to a beer. He pops the tab, taking a big, messy slug. Amber liquid trickles down his chin. He's wasted, I think.

"Thought about what?" I ask, buttoning my jeans. My fingers shake just slightly. James' sudden intrusion startled me. It's midday, and he's supposed to be at his desk in Portland's so-called Silicon Forest, answering phone calls from corporate hotshots who can't seem to access their email. He's dressed for it; he's even wearing his lanyard with his name and photo on it.

"Being more than this," James replies, sitting on my futon. He puts his feet up on my rickety coffee table, jerry-rigged out of weathered, wooden crates. They groan under his weight.

His abrupt movements jostle his beer, and a thin trickle of foam edges down the back of his knuckles. He doesn't seem to notice, or rather, he doesn't seem to care. The liquid soaks the cuff of his dress shirt.

"I don't understand what you're talking about," I say.

"Think about it…we're apex predators, aren't we? We're at the top of the food chain, twice over. Why do we pretend to be just like them?" He taps his fingers

on the armrest, as if unable to sit still. He's excited about something.

"'Them?' James, I don't have time for this. I have a shift at the restaurant in a half an hour, and I still have to catch the bus." I reach for my purse, looping the thin strap over my shoulder. "We can talk later."

He says nothing, his eyes unfocused. I take that as acquiescence, stepping over his outstretched legs to reach the front door. But he grabs my wrist, pulling me down onto the futon beside him.

"Humans," he replies. He smells like beer, the menthol cigarettes he favors, and old sweat. Up close, I can see dark, wet patches under his arms.

"Are you high?" I yelp.

"I've been thinking about it a lot," he continues, breathless. "Maybe we're meant to eat them."

I wonder if I should call Angus. But he'll be asleep now; he worked a nightshift at Providence Med. I heard him get in early this morning before I had even gotten out of bed. Our apartments are divided by only a knot of piping, sandwiched between two sheets of thin drywall. His key scraping the lock woke me, and their raised voices kept me awake afterward. They were fighting, I think. Though, I couldn't make out the words. It sounded like thunder rolling in the distance. I could almost feel the change in barometric pressure.

"What did you take?" I ask. "Are you sick?" I press my palm against his forehead, but he slaps my hand away.

"Leigh! Have you ever noticed how they smell*?"*

"Jay, you are freaking me out. Seriously." I don't like what he's saying. It's barbaric, disgusting. I have

friends who are human, lovers, even. I've never once thought of them as less than—as sustenance. My human friend, Eric, was at my apartment just last night. We made eggplant parmesan and watched The Crown *on Netflix. He put his arm around me on the couch, and he smelled like Old Spice. Later, in my bed, I could smell the garlic and thyme clinging to his hair from the tomato sauce we had to take turns stirring as it simmered on the stovetop so it wouldn't boil over.*

"I'm certain of this," James says, rising from the couch. He sets his beer on the coffee table, ignoring the stack of cork coasters.

I hurriedly pick up his can, wiping at the wet ring left behind with my palm. The moisture simply spreads. I'll need a dish towel. I look up to admonish my twin, but he's gone. He left the door open.

Later that night, I hear Angus and James yelling at one another. The door slams, seeming to rattle the entire warehouse, and I can hear someone trotting down the metal stairs to the ground floor. After hours of silence, I'm woken up by the sound of more fighting, the television's squawk, and finally, a vicious snarl.

The Fish and Wildlife officer examines my license. "Volkov, huh? Is that Ukrainian?"

"Russian," I reply, trying to sound casual. "My parents immigrated from St. Petersburg in the eighties."

"You're quite far from Portland, aren't you? Vacationing here in Virginia?" He's asking a lot of questions. I wish he would just write my damn ticket and send me on my way.

"Something like that," I reply, shifting from foot to foot. The sky is a pale blue now, the low-hanging sun already scorching the asphalt. It will be a blisteringly hot day. In Wharton, I would spend days like this at the beach, jogging into the foaming breakers to cool my sun-burnished skin.

"Let me run this, then you can get out of here," the officer says, tipping the bill of his baseball cap. I lean against my car while he steps over to his truck. It's idling two spaces down from mine, its engine a low grumble. He keeps the door open, pulling a laptop out of the glove compartment. I catch a brief glimpse of a license database on the screen.

Volkov, huh? You're quite far from Portland.

"Shit," I breathe. As far as Law Enforcement knows, James Volkov is alive and is still the prime suspect in the yet-unsolved Nedry murder. I've seen the grainy image of my brother on the television more times than I can count. His pixelated visage is a constant fixture in true crime entertainment. I even heard a podcast episode about the so-called Portland Cannibal, a criminal profiler insinuating that James was insecure, craving intimacy.

Stop him. If the officer connects me to James, I'll inevitably be detained. I'll be questioned, and perhaps, I'll be arrested as an accomplice. After all, I crossed state lines with a fugitive. "Excuse me?" I call. My voice sounds too shrill.

The officer leans slightly out of the pickup so he can meet my eyes. "What's up?" I can see that he's filled out the requisite fields, his cursor hovering over the search bar.

"I don't feel well, I think I—" I slump against my car, my forearms on the hood. "—I'm going to faint." I can hear him getting out of the truck, something opening and closing with a hollow *thwump,* the gravel crunching as he approaches.

"It's the heat," he soothes. "Here's some water." He presses a cool plastic water bottle into my hand. He must have a cooler in his truck bed. "Come sit down. I have some food, too."

I grip the water bottle tightly, the plastic crinkling. "Thanks," I mumble, allowing him to steer me toward the back of his vehicle. He unlatches the back, gesturing for me to take a seat on the tailgate. There is indeed a Coleman cooler, and he retrieves a clementine from its icy berth.

When he holds it out to me, I grab his wrist and twist. I'm not quite strong enough to break it, but fur is already sprouting on my knuckles. As my hand contorts into a claw, the bone in his wrist splinters. He howls, the clementine rolling across the asphalt, leaving behind a dark, wet smear.

I've never hurt a human before. The man's eyes—wide, the eyelids spasmodic—remind me of the white-tailed deer I hunted in Bayou Sauvage with Luka. We would drive them toward the brackish marshes, knowing they would balk at the bank. After all, there were alligators just beneath the murky depths.

The man escapes my grip while I am in mid-transformation and flees. He's screaming now, cradling his wrist against his broad chest. I drop to all four paws, giving chase. I catch him before he makes it to the trailhead, leaping atop his back. He falls heavily, his face striking the pavement with a sickening *crunch*.

For a moment, he goes still—silent. I've knocked him unconscious.

For a moment, I consider mercy.

I can destroy his laptop while he's knocked out, then toss the hard drive into the swamp. He's wearing a wedding ring, the burnished gold band glinting. He was kind; he offered me a snack. He's the kind of person who carries snacks—perhaps he's a parent. James and I used to laugh at our mother because she always had a snack in her purse, no matter the occasion or how old we were. At a family wedding, she quietly offered me a Ziplock of cashews and dried fruit while we waited for the bride to walk down the aisle. *It's another two hours until dinner, lapochka.*

"Was it how you imagined?" I ask James, looking at him in the rear-view mirror. He's wolfish, per Angus' orders, though there's nothing discrete about an inky-black beast who's pointed ears brush against the ceiling.

We're on I-84, near Boise, and the others are asleep. Angus dozes in the passenger seat, his cheek flat against the windowpane. His flesh squeaks against the smooth surface whenever I brake too hard. Luka has slipped the shoulder strap of his seatbelt off, laying sideways across the backseat. He uses James' furred haunch as a pillow.

The enormous wolf meets my eyes in the mirror. We have the same eyes. "It was better," he murmurs, keeping his voice low. "Leigh, it was better than anything."

The officer suddenly comes to, his face warping into a grimace. He's crying now. "Please, puh-please," he blubbers. "Let5 me go, let me—"

I sink my teeth into his thick shoulder, and when he punches at my snout with shaking fists, causing sunspots to burst before my eyes, I rip his arm off.

CHAPTER EIGHT
(CANDY)

———— ⊲◆⊳ ————

"**C**andace Bailey." Hunter stomps into my apartment without knocking, the spare key in his fist. "What is going on with you?"

Lounging on my couch, hand midway inside a Smartfood popcorn bag, I give him a quizzical look. "I'm pretty sure you're violating some sort of tenant's rights law barging in here."

"I'm worried about you," Hunter murmurs, sitting on the couch beside me. "First the outburst at mom's memorial and now calling out of work?"

When I woke up this morning, I couldn't bear the thought of serving coffee with a grotesque smile plastered on my face. I called out with every intention of writing, but I haven't even opened my laptop.

"It wasn't an *outburst*," I sniff. "Pardon me for not wanting to rehash my grief for the hundredth time." After the memorial I felt flayed open, a thousand paper cuts revealing my insides to the open air. In the alleyway behind Ebb and Flow, I sobbed, pouring errant pebbles out of my Payless heels. Upstairs, I poured myself into a hot bath, smoking a joint Julien had left behind until my brain felt fuzzy.

Hunter sighs. "You could have talked to me, Cay."

I'm not entirely sure I could have. Hunter's life has changed dramatically in the last twelve months. I barely fit into it. Between the remodel of the cafe, having to testify against Geoff Hawkins, and moving Angus into his bungalow, he hasn't had a spare moment. I only see him at work, wherein we exchange life updates between customers.

I roll up the popcorn bag and set it aside. "I'm sick," I add, an afterthought, forcing out a short, dry cough.

Hunter gives me a sidelong look. "Do you want me to bring you anything later? Emmanuel made some tomato bisque." He clearly doesn't believe I'm ill but is willing to play along.

"No. I'm not hungry." Before he rises, I grasp his wrist. "I'll make it up to you. I'll volunteer for inventory on Friday."

"Really?" Hunter's face brightens. "It'll be like the old days: just the Bailey kids." I can't help but to think about the long, hazy nights folding t-shirts in the back of the shop, listening to Red Hot Chili Peppers on the radio. Back then, Hunter and I were teens and Ebb and Flow sold personalized clothing and chotskies.

Once Hunter leaves, I peel myself off the couch. I can't sit here anymore, stagnating. In my bedroom, I dress in a pair of jeans, holes worn in the knees, and a cropped t-shirt. I scrape my hair back into a loose ponytail. Getting dressed does make me feel somewhat better. Slipping my feet into flip-flops, I head downstairs, taking the alleyway exit rather than walking through the cafe.

I am, after all, meant to be sick. Hunter knew I was telling a fib, but I shouldn't rub it in his face.

I'm not entirely sure where I'm heading. Instead, I meander down Main Street, window shopping. Outside Maisie's, the boutique, I stop to admire a sundress, cream-colored with sunflowers adorning the bodice. *I wonder if they have my size*. I step inside the store, waving at Gene behind the counter. He's an older man with an unwavering love for tropical prints. Today, he is wearing a Tommy Bahama button-down, covered in hibiscus flowers. The top three buttons are undone, revealing a tuft of silvery chest hair.

"Hey, Candy," he croons in his sing-song soprano.

"Hey, Gene," I reply, making a beeline toward the racks. "How's business?"

"Can't complain," he replies, resting his elbows on the countertop. He watches me thumb through the hangers. "I saw your brother out at the bar with that tall drink of water he's dating."

"Oh yeah?"

"Do you think it's serious?" Gene folds a stick of gum into his mouth. His hopeful tone makes me laugh.

"Very." I chuckle. I finally find the dress in an XL, draping it over my arm.

"A shame," Gene muses. "Something tells me that man could teach this old dog some new tricks."

"I'm going to go try this on," I snicker.

The dressing rooms are down a short hallway shrouded by a venetian curtain. The hallway is dim, lit only by the pinpoints of sunshine that bleed through the lace. A floral pattern dapples the far wall, my skin. It always makes me think of faerie circles, the portal to wonderland. There are three dressing rooms, each with its own slatted door. Only one appears to be occupied; I can see a shadow moving beyond the slats. I step into an unoccupied stall, hanging the dress on a hook.

I slip the dress on but can't reach the zipper in the back. I consider heading out to the front of the store, roving eyes be damned, so that Gene can help. But there's someone in the stall next to mine, isn't there? I rap on the wall with my knuckles. "Hey, so…this is awkward, but could you help me?"

The shuffling next door ceases, then a woman's voice floats through the thin wall. "Are you talking to me?"

"Yeah, I need someone to zip me up. Do you have a second?"

The woman is quiet for a long moment. I almost convince myself she never existed at all. But then, there's a soft knock on my door. I open it and look into the golden eyes of a stranger. The woman is dressed in a heather gray tunic and a pair of cutoff shorts, both with tags on them. Her feet are bare.

"Hi," I say.

"Hey," the woman replies, shifting uncomfortably from foot to foot. "You needed help?"

"Yeah." I turn around so she can see the zipper. I crane my neck to look over my shoulder. "I can't reach," I explain, an apology implicit therein. *I'm sorry to bother you.*

The woman hesitates for a moment, then slowly inches the zipper up my spine. Her hands are cold, the joint of her pointer finger sliding across my skin. Midway up my back, she pauses to sweep my hair out of the way, draping it over my shoulder. Her touch makes me shiver, and I look away, embarrassed. My cheeks grow hot. Can she see?

Finally, she completes the ascent. "All done," she announces. I turn toward her. "You look really pretty," she adds, "in that dress, I mean."

"Thanks," I manage. I hold out a hand. "I'm Candace—Candy."

She takes my hand, her grip loose. "I'm Haley," she replies. "Nice to meet you."

She's gorgeous. The thought bubbles up before I can stamp it down. I desperately want to keep talking to her, even though the very thought frightens me. "Are you here on vacation?" I ask. "I've never seen you around before."

"Something like that," she replies. Her eyes flick away from my face, as if afraid I can read her mind.

I wish I could. I'm intrigued by her. I realize, suddenly, that I haven't released her hand. I drop it, knotting my hands behind my back.

"Do you live here?" Haley asks.

"Born and raised."

"Maybe you can help me, then," Haley says, nearly bouncing on her toes in excitement. "I'm looking for a...friend. I'm also looking for a great lunch place. I'm *starving.*"

"My brother has a cafe a few doors down," I reply, trying not to sound too eager. "Ebb and Flow. It's mostly coffee, but there's soup and sandwiches too. We have a great mushroom and swiss panini." I lean close, as if sharing a secret. "And you're in luck. I get an employee discount."

"It's my lucky day." Haley grins, revealing dazzlingly white teeth. The canines are noticeably distinct: two keen points, reminiscent of a vampire's fangs. "I'd love to try it."

CHAPTER NINE
(HALEY)

―◁◆▷―

I rip the tags off my new outfit, handing them over to the man at the counter. "I'll wear these out," I announce. He looks a bit miffed but scans the barcodes. I drop the rest of my selections on the counter: a pair of jeans, three pairs of leggings, and several t-shirts.

"And your other clothes?" he asks, gesturing to the soiled shirt and jeans tucked under my arm. "Do you want a bag for them too?"

"No," I reply. "Could you toss them in the garbage for me?" He raises both eyebrows. "They're so last season," I explain, handing them over.

"It'll be $153.99," he says unceremoniously, dropping my clothes into the trash can beneath the counter. "Cash or credit?"

I hand him my credit card. As I sign my receipt, Candy steps out from behind the lacy curtain, shaking out her long hair. She smiles when she sees me, placing the sundress back on the rack.

"Not your style, Candy?" the man asks.

"A little short," she replies.

I am glad Candy and I are no longer in the cramped dressing room. All I could smell was her sun-burnished flesh, warm like freshly baked bread. *Why can't I stop thinking about consuming everything in my path?* It's as though the ink in which Samuel had written about his crimes had seeped into my pores, practically running through my veins, hot and viscous like an infection.

"Are you ready to go?" Candy asks me.

I nod, following her out to the street. I felt rudderless up until the moment Candy had asked for my help in the dressing room.

We walk side-by-side, making our way down the block. Main Street is crowded. Most of the pedestrians are wearing bathing suits, colorful towels taut around their waists or draped over their shoulders. The chemical odor of sunscreen combines with the briny sea air. It's as though Wharton has its own atmosphere.

"Where are you staying?" Candy asks.

"The Cove," I reply.

Candy wrinkles her nose. "That place is a dump. I'm genuinely shocked it's still open."

I shrug. "It's not so bad."

The bell tinkles when we step into Ebb and Flow. It's cool inside, smelling strongly of coffee beans and vanilla. Candy grasps my elbow, leaning close. "I forgot I called out sick," she whispers, her breath hot against my cheek.

I turn and give her a curious look. "Should we go somewhere else?"

"It'll be fine," she assures me. "But I'm going to get reamed."

When we approach the counter, a man with disheveled chestnut hair smiles warmly at me. "Welcome to Ebb and Flow, what can I get you?" He glances at Candy, his customer service smile flickering.

"This is my brother Hunter," Candy says in a stage-whisper. "He thinks I'm sick."

Hunter snorts. "I will let this slide since you're going to make it up to me," Hunter said. "But you have a lot of nerve."

I examine the chalkboard with its many sumptuous selections: paninis, bagels, baked pastries, various coffee selections. "Can I get a panini and a black coffee?"

"Sure," Hunter says. "We have mushroom and swiss, BLT, or ham and cheese."

"I've already heard such positive things about the mushroom and swiss," I say. "I *have* to try it."

"I'll get that started for you," Hunter says, reaching for a carafe of coffee. He pours it into a paper cup, pressing the lid on with a practiced hand. "Ten dollars, even."

"I've got it," Candy says before I can grab my wallet. "Add a cobb salad, would you?" She hands her brother a twenty-dollar bill.

"You don't have to do that," I stammer.

"Nonsense." Candy grins. "I insist." After Hunter rings us up, Candy leads me to a small cafe-style table. I sit, cupping my coffee cup between my palms.

"Thank you," I say, "for lunch."

Candy blushes again, the rosy hue creeping down her swan-like neck. "Don't mention it. Blame it on that Wharton hospitality."

Hunter brings us our meals, both plates balanced on one arm. "Enjoy," he says. I take a bite of my panini, delighting at the way the nutty, creamy cheese compliments the earthy mushrooms.

"I'm actually in town looking for some—" I begin, but the words turn to ash on my tongue. Suddenly, I am inundated with the smell of petrichor, the forest floor after a gentle rain. It is overpowering, deadening even the smell of the sandwich in my hand. It's a smell I've always associated with wolfishness. It's altogether different from the meaty smell of humans.

"Hey, Candy." A burly man with dark, shoulder-length hair drapes his arm around Hunter's neck. "And who is this?" His eyes meet mine, his head tilting just slightly.

"This is Haley," Candy chirps. "We met at Maisie's."

"*What* are you?" the man asks. His eyebrows furrow.

"Excuse me?" I stammer.

"What are you in town for?" he asks. "Business or pleasure?"

I glance at Candy and Hunter. Had they noticed? But no, they hadn't; Candy is eating, Hunter is nodding at a passing customer, wishing them a good afternoon.

"Pleasure," I reply. "Just a short vacation." His blue eyes bore holes into mine, but I don't dare look away.

"I'm Angus," the man says, offering his hand to shake. "Angus Chilton."

"Nice to meet you," I reply. He's still staring at me, and when our hands clasp, he squeezes tightly. I turn my attention to Candy. "Is there a bathroom here?" I ask meekly.

"Yeah," she says, gesturing to a small, narrow hallway. "Just down there."

I pop out of my seat. "Thanks," I manage, speed-walking into the relative privacy of the hall. There are two bathroom doors therein: both labeled unisex. I push into one, feeling as though I can't breathe. Angus made me feel so exposed, like he could see every one of my indiscretions outlined on my face.

Suddenly, a large hand grasps my hair, shoving me hard into the small room. I slam against the sink, the porcelain punching the air out of my lungs. I spin around and find myself toe-to-toe with Angus Chilton. He crowds the space, forcing me on my tiptoes. "What are you?" he repeats. He slams his palm against the mirror, leaning close to press his nose against my neck. "You smell like me," he continues.

My teeth crowd my mouth, and a growl grumbles out of my chest. I push him backward, and his eyes widen in surprise; I'm stronger than he expected. "Don't touch me." I swallow, hoping to push the wolfishness down and away like a lump in my throat.

Angus locks the bathroom door. "This is my town," he says coolly. "I'm the Alpha here." There's a threat there. He bares his teeth, showing me two rows of long, sharp daggers. I know what those teeth can do. I've seen what mine did to Tara.

Oh, Tara. I can't shake the image of her hand resting on the carpet, her fingers curled. It was the same hand that touched my ear, that rested upon my hip as we swayed to the music.

71

"I'm not here to cause trouble," I reply. "I think…I came here looking for you." My heart is hammering. I'm frightened, but I don't want him to know that.

"Me?"

"I was looking for someone called Blanchard." The bathroom is tiny and airless. I am keenly aware of the paresthesia coursing up and down the nape of my neck as the fur erupts and abates, erupts and abates. I grit my teeth. "Someone named Rafe."

Angus surveys me, expressionless. "Rafe Blanchard was my grandfather. He died before I was born."

The tile beneath my feet seems to tilt; I feel off-balance. *What will I do now?* I can't go back to Ridgerton. "Oh," I croak.

"Why?" Angus asks. "Why are you looking for him?"

I don't want to say. If I speak the words aloud, the wolf inside of me will hear. She is an entity that can be summoned. Thinking of her as divorced from me is the only way I've made it this far without crumbling. *She did this. It wasn't me. Help me stop her!*

"It was a mistake to come here," I say, side-stepping him and unlocking the door in one swift motion. "I'm sorry." The sounds of the cafe rush into my ears, replacing the *thump-a-thump* of my heart. Angus doesn't follow me as I stride toward the table.

Candy smiles at me. She is radiant, sun-kissed. "So," she says, drawing the word out as though it's part of a song. "Do you have any plans for the rest of the day?"

I sink into my seat, staring at my half-eaten sandwich. My appetite is gone. "No," I say. Out of the corner of my eye, I watch Angus ease out of the hallway. I can feel his eyes on me, and my skin burns. I try to focus on Candy's face, the dimple in her cheek.

"Well," Candy says, "maybe we could go to the beach? That is, if you want company." She spears a bit of tomato. When she pops it into her mouth, juice trickles down her chin, reminding me of blood. *She wants to spend more time with me!* I should be elated, but Angus has rattled me.

"I think I'm just going to head back to the hotel," I mumble. "I'm tired." I offer her a wan smile. "Thank you for lunch."

Candy's brow furrows. "Are you okay? You don't look so good, and you've hardly touched your food."

"Yeah. I'm sorry, I have to go." I jolt to my feet and nearly jog out of the cafe, the bell jingling overhead. On the street, I collide with a passerby, and I shout my apologies over my shoulder. A half block from the cafe I break into a run.

CHAPTER TEN
(ANGUS)

————◁◆▷————

I don't have an opportunity to ask Hunter about Candy's new friend until we are in bed. As he slides between the bedsheets, I prop myself up on my elbow. "Did that girl seem strange to you? The one having lunch with your sister."

"Not particularly," Hunter replies. He runs his hand through his hair, pushing it off his forehead. I lean over and kiss the smooth skin there.

I weigh whether to tell him. I often find him staring at the spot in the cafe where James had died, his eyes glassy. When he testified at Geoff's trial, he was plagued by nightmares for weeks afterward. While he's accepting of me, wolf pelt and all, he has been through more than his fair share. This is a wolfish matter, not a human one. Still—

"She's like me," I say. "I could smell her."

Hunter sits up. "Really?" His eyebrows rise toward his hairline. "We should tell Candy, shouldn't we? What if—"

I shush him, pressing a finger against his petal-soft lips. I can feel the curve of his frown. "I took care of it," I assure him. "She ran off. It *seems* like she came to see me, or rather, my grandfather."

"Your grandfather?"

"I'm just as confused as you are," I admit. "He's been dead since 1958."

For me, Rafe Chilton is little more than a photograph on the wall in my grandmother's house. It sits on the end table beside Ama's favorite wingback armchair, cloistered in a simple, gilded frame. The corner of the frame has been worn down to the raw wood beneath because Ama always runs her fingers over it when she passes by. It's a reflex, I think, but it was clearly born of a desperate longing.

"Maybe you should ask Ama," Hunter suggests. "How is she?"

I sigh. Ama has been plagued by bouts of pneumonia. "She waves me away when I ask," I admit. "She doesn't want to be a bother, and she *certainly* doesn't want me to bring up moving in again."

The last time I asked, Ama jabbed her finger against my sternum, her sharp nail leaving a half-moon tear in my t-shirt and indenting the flesh beneath. *I'll die in this house, child,* she had said. *I'll die in my own bed, looking out at the same beach I've looked at for seventy years.*

Hunter chuckles. "She's an independent lady," he says. "Are you sure I shouldn't worry about that woman hanging around my sister?"

"I don't think so, love," I assure him, covering his mouth with mine. "I'll keep an eye on her." Before he

75

can protest—I can almost *feel* the questions bouncing on the flat of his tongue—I slip my hands beneath the comforter and make him burn.

The walk to Ama's bungalow is short, but by the time I arrive, sweat soaks my shirt collar. The light cotton clings to my back, and I peel it away. It's an unseasonably humid day, and it feels as though the air is soupy. The gravel crunches beneath my tennis shoes, announcing my arrival. The lacy curtain in Ama's front window flutters; she's spotted me.

I wait on the porch for her, leaning against the railing. It sags a bit beneath my weight. I'll have to replace it soon. I mentally add it to my perpetually expanding to-do list, just behind replacing the light fixture in her alley kitchen.

A mosquito buzzes around my head, drawn to the briny smell of my sweat, and I slap it away when it alights on my neck.

"Angus," Ama says by way of greeting, easing open the front door. She looks particularly frail today, dressed in high-waisted linen pants and a boat-neck tee. I can see the sharp edges of her clavicle, the dark hollows tucked into its curve. Her skin is a bit gray. I worry that if she is in the sun for too long, she will turn to cinder.

"Granny," I reply, leaning down and kissing her cool cheeks, one after the other. "How are you feeling?"

Ama lets me lead her to the small wrought-iron garden bench beneath the awning. While her expression is impassive, she shakes my hand. Her arthritis is acting up, every joint grinding in its socket. "I wish you wouldn't ask me that," she mutters.

I sit beside her. "It's a valid question."

"I'm an old woman, child. I feel *old*."

I chuckle. "I'm working on the back deck today," I tell her, "but first, I want to ask you about something."

"As long as it's not about my health," she warns me, showing me a mouth full of jagged teeth. It is meant to be a threat, but it reminds me of a growling, spitting chihuahua.

"It's about a young woman. I think her name was Haley. She's in town, asking about Rafe Blanchard." At the mention of her late husband's name, Ama's lupine ears swivel toward me. Her blue eyes—oceans that have become murky with cataracts—bore into mine. I have her attention.

"What did you say?"

"She's looking for grandpa. I told her he is dead, and she freaked out—ran off," I continue. "She didn't tell me why."

Ama presses her chapped lips together. It's strange to see her without lipstick. *Had I forgotten it on my last grocery trip? No*, I assure myself, I hadn't. I remember lingering in the cosmetics aisle, straining to read the tiny labels. She wanted a Clinique shade called clove-*something*, and I had to ask a store employee to help me find it.

She sits quietly for a long moment, her eyes half-lidded. A seagull, nesting up in the eaves, lets out a sharp *squawk*, rusting its wings. The mosquito returns,

77

tickling my earlobes. "I know that name," she finally murmurs. "Come inside, Angus. Let me show you."

Inside, the bungalow is stifling, the air seeming to stagnate. A young woman sits on the couch, her bare heels on the coffee table. "Hey, Angus," she says, resting her palms on her round belly. "Can you *please* convince Ama to turn the air conditioner on? This baby is going to boil alive."

I smile at her.

"Open a window, Toby," Ama grunts, opening a large chest in the corner. She hefts an armful of quilts out of it, setting them aside. The smell of mothballs fills the air.

Toby sighs and gives me a pleading look. Poor thing. She's nearly six months pregnant and sweat beads on her forehead. I wordlessly reach for the thermostat, lowering the temperature by five degrees.

She mouths, *thank you.*

I sit beside the younger woman. "How are you feeling, Toby?" I ask.

"Enormous." Sheshe chuckles. "I hate not being able to run with you and the pack."

The pack. I was a lone wolf for months after Leigh and Luka left. But, as is the custom, other wolves gravitated toward Wharton—and me. It's as though there's an invisible wire knotted between all of us, tugging us toward each other. Wolves are rarely ever alone. Toby was the first, her belly leading the way. Renner walked into Ebb and Flow six weeks later, blown in by a squall on the coast. His houseboat is docked just behind Hunter and mine's bungalow now. Finally, Alexandre came just two weeks ago. He's nearly as old as Ama and calls her *ma belle femme*. She calls him *le petit ennui*.

"Here it is," Ama announces. She walks over, carrying an enormous leatherbound book. She sits on the other side of me, dropping the book onto my lap. She flips to the last page. Under a sleeve of clear plastic, there's a photo of an old man and a baby. "I think," Ama says, resting her finger on the baby's visage, "this is the girl you've met."

It's difficult to tell. There is some resemblance, but babies are so amorphous, they can resemble anyone.

"And this," she strokes the cheek of the old man, "this is my friend, Samuel."

CHAPTER ELEVEN
(LEIGH)

⊲◆⊳

I prowl the motel breezeway, searching for a snack machine. I haven't eaten since dawn, and the sun had set hours ago. The sky is an inky blue-black, the air as thick as velvet. The only reprieve from the oppressive humidity is the breeze coming off the ocean, made cool by the perpetually brisk seawater. I practically sleep-walked into Wharton, high off what I had done to the man in the swamp.

James was right. Of course, he was right.

"You should have seen this *girl,* bro," a man chortles from behind me, making me jump. He walks past me, his flip-flops slapping against the concrete. In one hand, he holds his iPhone, and in the other, a Styrofoam takeout container.

A tinny voice floats from the phone's speaker: "Did you hit it, dawg?"

"Nah," the man replies, unable to conceal the disappointment in his voice. "She wouldn't put out. Frigid cunt." He glances at me and falters, offering me a toothy grin. I can see my reflection in his aviator sunglasses perched on his sweaty forehead.

"Where'd you get that?" I ask, pointing at his takeout container. It smells phenomenal: piquant and oleaginous. My stomach rumbles.

"Dottie's," he replies.

"What?" his iPhone asks.

He opens the lid, showing me a hamburger, its bun glossy, and a nest of French fries with granules of coarse salt glittering.

"Looks *good.*" I nearly moan when I say it, and his grin widens.

"I'm about to go to my room and finish this, maybe have a few shots of Malibu," the man says, licking at his lips. "Want to come?"

"What?" his iPhone repeats.

The guy abruptly ends the call with a swipe of his finger. The phone disappears into the deep pocket of his Bermuda shorts.

I'm so hungry. My stomach clenches tight like a fist, almost heady with need. It's as though I haven't eaten in days. "Sure," I say brazenly, taking the container from his hands. "Let's go."

The stranger's room is on the far side of the motel. It's a mirror image of mine, but far more lived in: the bed is unmade, a surfboard leans against the wall, toiletries litter the countertop, and damp towels hang over the rumbling air conditioner.

"I'm Colson," the man announces.

"Nice to meet you, Colson," I reply.

"Do you often have dinner with strangers?" he asks.

"No." I laugh, sitting on the edge of the bed, the takeout container in my lap. "I'm just *very* hungry." I feel heady, driven senseless by desire.

Colson paws through a bag, pulling out a bottle of banana rum. He unscrews the top, taking a swig. His Adam's apple bobs. "Want some?" he asks when he comes up for air. He wipes his mouth with the back of his hand.

I take the bottle and tip it back, swallowing the noxious liquid. My fingers and toes grow pleasantly warm. I take another swig, then hand it back.

Colson places the bottle on the floor and sits beside me, reaching for a fry. "You're really pretty," he murmurs, leaning close. His banana breath is hot on my cheek.

I take a fry and pop it in my mouth. It's lukewarm and soggy. The hunger doesn't abate. I reach for another, but I know it will be as appealing as a mouthful of sawdust. Colson's lips press brusquely against my cheekbone. I haven't been smelling the burger and fries at all, but rather, his flesh: greasy and over-salted.

My gums itch.

No! I feel as though I am slowly being torn in half. I am of two minds: the first, horrified, longing to run away; the second, sick with desire. The girl and the wolf vying for a foothold. Colson dangles between us, like bait on a hook. Still—

James was right.

Colson takes the takeout container off my lap, placing it on the carpet beside the rum. "Didn't you hear what I said?" he asks. He kisses my mouth, his tongue insistently probing between my parted lips.

I am dimly aware that he is roughly squashing my breast through my shirt. I tangle my fingers in his shaggy, dishwater blond hair pulling him close. I kiss his stubbly neck, dragging the flat of my tongue up its length. My eyes roll. *Delicious.*

Colson lays back on the blankets, pulling me astride his hips. His eyes are two round saucers; he can't believe his good luck. He grasps my ass, grinding his pelvis against mine. "Take your shirt off," he says gruffly.

I nip his lip with razor-sharp teeth.

He hisses in pain. "You bit me!" he exclaims. Colson holds me at arm's length, his eyebrows knitted together. A tiny rivulet of blood trickles down his chin. "You kinky bitch!"

I can taste his blood in my mouth. I lick at my teeth, desperate to swallow every drop of him. Paresthesia crawls up the back of my arms. I look down at my hands, fingers splayed on his chest, and watch in fascination as my nails thicken and grow. Colson is speaking again, but I'm not listening. I tilt my chin toward the ceiling, staring at the oscillating ceiling fan. The hunger roils, nausea coating my mouth with thick slobber. A dull rumbling fills my ears. It's the sound of the bones in my face crunching, contorting, shearing against one another like tectonic plates.

Colson's hands rest on my thighs, his thumbs drawing concentric circles beneath the hem of my cut-offs. His eyes are closed, and he mutters to himself in a breathy sing-song voice. I catch only bits and pieces.

He's describing just how he's going to fuck a kinky bitch like me. I pull my lips away from my jaws, a nightmarish grin.

"Colson," I breathe. My voice is deeper now, textured like broken glass.

When he opens his eyes, he stiffens beneath me. "What the *fu*—" he manages, before I close my jaws on his windpipe, squeezing tight. *Goodnight, Colson.*

Afterward, in my own room, I run a bath. I feel out of it, floating, bobbing near the popcorn ceiling. I hum to myself, giggling. It's like being drunk, like being fucked into a stupor. I sink into the tub, delighting when the rust-colored blood drying on my skin turns the hot water pink.

I am full. I pat my distended stomach as I hum. It feels good not to contend with the yearning anymore. I scrub the blood off my skin, using my nails. When I am pink and new, I let the water drain. Wrapping a towel beneath my armpits, I swipe the steam off the mirror. My reflection stares back at me, and for a moment, I don't recognize her. She's soft, unblemished. and unbothered. There's nary a wrinkle or bag to be seen. It's as if that one horrific act was a miracle salve.

I pad into the bedroom, dressing in fresh underwear and a t-shirt. I brought the Malibu from Colson's room, and it sits on my nightstand. Flecks of blood adorn the white bottle, and I am careful not to touch them when I take a glug. I wince; it tastes like banana candy set ablaze, thick, gooey, and fiery.

Dimly, I am aware of sirens. They scream into the parking lot, flooding the breezeway with red and blue lights. The colors seep through the half-closed curtains, throwing faerie lights on the ceiling. That didn't take long.

Though, I did make quite the mess.

CHAPTER TWELVE
(CANDY)

———◁◆▷———

During my shift, I catch myself thinking about Haley. Each time, I startle as if caught with my hand deep inside the cookie jar. The thought propagates slowly, sneaking up on my consciousness like a predator in the grass. As I loop caramel syrup on top of a Frappuccino, I find myself thinking about her amber eyes. When I pull a cinnamon roll from the pastry case, swaddling it in parchment paper, I think of her sweet smile, the light smattering of cocoa-colored freckles across the bridge of her nose.

"Have you seen Haley since yesterday?" Hunter asks, wiping his damp hands on a dish towel. "She sure left in a rush."

"No," I reply, unable to contain the disappointment in my voice.

"Maybe it's for the best," Hunter says, shrugging his thin shoulders. It's a strange thing to say. But, before I can respond, more customers trickle into the cafe. With them comes an acrid odor, reminiscent of a smoldering campfire.

"Is that a *fire*?" I skirt around the counter, craning my neck to peer down the street. Gray smoke curls up into the sky, commingling with the clouds above, but it's difficult to discern its point of origin; I can only see so far.

"That shitty motel," a customer answers, over-hearing. "We passed it on the way here."

The Cove! Isn't that where Haley is staying? Electricity trickles down the base of my skull, and I lurch toward the door. "I'm going on break," I call over my shoulder.

"Can—" Hunter says, but I've already compressed the push bar and stepped out onto the sidewalk.

A breeze ruffles my hair. It smells like a woodstove. I trot down the block, skirting around pedestrians and a cavalcade of sidewalk signs touting sales, free WIFI, and the like.

When the motel finally meanders into view, I sigh in relief. There has been a fire, but it appears to have been small, affecting only a fraction of the u-shaped building. Ash coats the parking lot like freshly fallen snow. I leave footprints from the sidewalk all the way to the crisscross of yellow police tape.

I spot a familiar face in the crowd, a guy from my creative non-fiction seminar. Paul watches the firefighters, turning a small spiral bound notebook around and around in his hands. "What happened?" I ask him.

"Some tourist was smoking cigarettes in his room," he replies, "torched his room and the empty one next to it."

"Is anyone hurt?" From my vantage point, I can just barely see into the soot-covered room. The roof had collapsed into it, ceiling tiles and ductwork piled on the bedspread.

"I don't know," Paul replies. "There was an ambulance here, but it left a while ago. Its lights and sirens were off." I watch the firemen file in and out of the room, a colony of yellow ants. The building groans under their footfalls, the drywall shuddering. "This might be the end for the Cove," Paul continues. "I doubt anyone will fork over the money to fix it back up."

But I'm not listening—not really. Haley is here, too, standing near the front office with a gaggle of other tourists. A rotund man in khaki shorts shouts about his room, reeking of smoke. "This has *ruined* our entire vacation," he cries. I catch her eye and offer her a tight smile. Though, I think it may better resemble a grimace. I feel awkward, as if I've been shoved under a hot, white spotlight and discovered I hadn't learned my lines.

She smiles back.

I wind my way through the dwindling crowd. Most of the rubberneckers have been on their way, heading to wherever they were going before the smoke signal summoned their interest. After all, there's nothing to see; one can only look at the charred remains of Room Twenty-three for so long. "I hope that wasn't *your* room," I remark when I'm within earshot.

"No, I'm on the other side," Haley replies, jerking her thumb over her shoulder. Up close, I notice the flesh beneath her eyes is droopy and grey. She gnaws at her bottom lip, leaving behind a red bloom. "Though, they're kicking me out. Something about structural integrity."

"I was thinking about you," I say, before I realize how it sounds. My cheeks burn, and I press my palms against them as if it will snuff out my own fire. "I mean, I saw the smoke, and I wanted to make sure you're okay."

Haley smiles. "That's really sweet, Candy." The way she says my name makes me feel almost feverish. *Can,* as though asking a tentative question, then *dee,* a firm tap of her tongue against her teeth.

"What are you going to do now?" I ask, though it's not quite the question I want to ask.

She sighs, leaning against the stucco wall. "I'm not sure. I've already called the Great Inn, and they're still booked solid. Maybe I'll stay somewhere outside of town or just go home." She looks so dejected, as if the thought is too much to bear.

Haley had said she was looking for someone, hadn't she? *I'm looking for a...friend. I'm also looking for a great lunch place.* I had helped her with the latter, but perhaps I can do something about the former, too. "You haven't finished your business in town, right?" I say, the words spilling out at my feet. "Why not just stay at my place?"

"Really?" Haley's amber eyes bore into mine. She tentatively touches my elbow, her fingertips just barely brushing against my flesh. I try to ignore the way it makes the baby hairs on my skin stand straight up.

"Sure," I say, "I mean, you'd have to sleep on a couch. But it's a comfortable couch."

"Candy," Haley breathes, "that would be incredible. I was so worried I would have to go home without—" she pauses, licking at her lips. "—without finishing what I came here to do."

"Maybe I can help you out with that too," I offer.

"Maybe," Haley agrees, though she doesn't sound too terribly convinced. "Let me go get my bags." We walk together along the breezeway, crowded with motel residents. She opens the door to Room Six. Inside, the room smells faintly of smoke. Her clothes are draped on the table, with no suitcase in sight. Then, Haley mutters in apology, "I didn't really *pack.*"

She certainly didn't. The majority of her clothing still has the Marnie's Boutique price tag attached.

"You must have been in a hurry," I observe.

"Something like that." Haley disappears into the bathroom, returning with a toothbrush, a travel-sized tube of toothpaste, and the tiny shampoo and conditioner bottles provided by the motel. "It's a long story," she adds, an afterthought. She hands me the toiletries, tosses the motel room keycard onto the bed, and gathers the clothing in her arms.

CHAPTER THIRTEEN
(HALEY)

———⊲◆▷———

As soon as we cross the threshold, Candy is a dervish. She picks up empty takeout containers, protein bar wrappers, scribbled post-its, and the like, dumping them into an overfilled trash can. She ducks her head as she works, seemingly embarrassed, her gingery hair covering her face.

I set my pile of belongings down onto the couch. "Your apartment is really nice," I offer, hoping to soothe her.

"Hardly." She laughs. She dumps a final load into the can, punching it down with her fists. "Though, I'm sure it beats the Cove. I've heard *stories* about that place."

I wander around the perimeter of the loft. The majority of the space is devoted to living: consisting of an overstuffed couch, a flat-screen television, a coffee table laden with books and notebooks, and a record player perched atop a milk crate. The kitchen occupies one corner, detached from the living space by a woodblock island. The bedroom area is in the

91

opposite corner. I can just see the edge of a bed, mostly hidden behind a four-paneled room divider covered in Japanese cranes and cherry blossoms. I resist the urge to peer behind the divider, though I really would like to see Candy's bedroom. There's something so intimate about a bedroom.

I think of my own bedroom, stacked high with boxes I never unpacked. Even so, a viewer would have known me quite well, just by glancing through the door. They would know I slept fitfully, all my pillows having been squeezed and wrenched from their cases. They would know I drink coffee to keep myself awake, because I've left several mugs on the bedside table. They would know I have a secret, the lump of Samuel Campbell's diary raising the mattress off its frame.

Candy finally settles on the couch, stacking the items on the coffee table into a neat little pile. "I'm working on a big assignment for my MFA," she says. "It's made me a little *distracted*. I'm not usually this messy."

"You're a writer?" I ask, sitting beside her.

"Someone has to write to be a writer." She chuckles. "So, no, I'm not." Candy wakes her laptop with a key-press, showing me an empty Word document. "I once had an undergrad professor tell me I can't be a writer because I haven't lived long enough. Maybe he's right."

"If that was true, all of the best literature would be written by ninety-year-olds."

Candy tucks a strand of auburn hair behind her ear. "I've got to return downstairs. I'm well past my thirty-minute lunch break, and Hunter will be furious." She rises, stepping over my legs and heads to the front door. "Make yourself at home. There's alcohol and water in the fridge. The remote is on the tv stand. I can bring back dinner."

"Thank you," I murmur, "for letting me stay."

"Of course." Candy grins. "I'll be off at 6 o'clock."

The room smells like her perfume long after she leaves. It's a unique fragrance with peppery top notes and a floral undercurrent. I find it later, sitting on the edge of the bathroom sink: a small, creamy-pink *Glossier* bottle. After the sounds of her footfalls fade, I reach for the remote, turning on the television.

It's early in the afternoon, and the local alphabet affiliates are news centric. After a story about the latest iPhone and a weather report ("sunshine, and lots of it!"), the Breaking News chyron sweeps across the bottom quarter of the screen. "Firefighters have made a grisly discovery at The Cove Motel, the site of a devastating fire. A man, identified as Colton Hess, was found deceased beneath the bed in Room Twenty-Three. It is unclear whether he hid there to escape the blaze or was put there by an unknown assailant."

The news anchor presses her lips together, shuffling the pages in her hand. "Law enforcement believe Hess may have died as a result of injuries sustained before the fire, including what can only be described as a bite on his neck."

A bite.

My mouth floods with saliva. I can't help but to think of how Tara's skin buckled in my mouth, blood surging from each puncture wound. When I swallow, I imagine it is hot and viscous like blood fresh from the vein. Hunger sits like a weight in my stomach, and suddenly, I am aware of Candy's scent on the couch cushions.

I lurch to my feet.

"No," I say aloud, startling myself. My voice is a plaintive whimper, inordinately loud in the quiet room. I stumble into the bathroom, dropping to my knees next to the toilet. I feel as though I may be sick. My stomach ratchets into a tight ball, burning acid sloshing up my esophagus. I gag.

Fur covers the back of my hands, and I rip at it with my nails. If the wolf won't leave me alone, then I'll remove her, hair by hair. It's futile. In seconds, my arms are covered in silvery-gray fur. "No!" I snarl, around a mouthful of lengthening teeth. I squeeze my eyes shut. *Breathe*.

In the living room, the news anchor continues, "Wharton residents will no doubt remember the serial murders in 1946 and 1947, when several victims were found with bite wounds. While Freddy Parnell died in prison in 1993, this reporter wonders whether this was a copycat attack."

My thoughts surge, sliding over one another like slippery eels. I can barely process one before it is replaced. Samuel was in Wharton in nearly the entirety of the 1940s, he said so in his diary. A man was murdered in the same hotel I slept in—

Did I sleep? I can't remember. I smelled smoke. I remember looking out the window, pressing my nose to the cool glass. I remember the glass growing foggy with my breath, the firetruck's lights resembling paint daubs. But what happened before that?

Maybe you killed him. I rear back away from the toilet, clasping my hands—paws—over my wolfish ears. But there's no quieting the thought, entrenched within my own cerebral cortex, Had I?

♦ ♦ ♦

There's a knock at the closed bathroom door. I open my eyes, my cheek resting on the cool, porcelain toilet seat. "I brought dinner," Candy says cheerily.

"I'll be right there!" I call. I clamber to my knees, then regain my feet. My reflection stares at me with red-rimmed eyes. I'm human again. I run my fingertips down the clamshell of my ear, baring my teeth to make certain they are blunt and square. Thankfully, I didn't transform entirely; my clothes are still intact, though the button of my shorts has popped off. The zipper holds them up well enough, and if I am careful, the hem of my shirt covers the stretched buttonhole.

The dark thoughts that plagued me have faded somewhat. "I didn't do it," I assure my reflection. "I was in my room, by myself, all night long."

Candy smiles when I walk into the living area. She's sitting on the couch, a plastic grocery bag on the coffee table. "How was your day?" she asks.

"It was okay," I fib. "I just watched television, mostly. I was too tired to go out."

Candy paws through the grocery bag, pulling out a pair of plastic-wrapped sandwiches, a container of cut fruit, and a small, cardboard box that she sets aside. "Dessert," she explains.

Wordlessly, I sit beside her. "This looks amazing."

"The perks of working in a cafe," she remarks. She picks up two sandwiches, cut into oblong triangles. "Which do you want? Egg salad or BLT?"

"BLT, please." She hands it over, and I carefully unwrap the sandwich. Candy opens the egg salad sandwich, taking a big bite. A bit of egg falls onto her lap, and she plucks it up, popping it into her mouth.

I nibble on the crust. I'm afraid to eat, as though it will unlock a deeper need in me.

"Did you see the news?" Candy asks, and my second bite tastes like ash.

"Yeah," I manage.

"Hunter is so anxious," Candy continues.

"Why?" I ask, forcing myself to take another bite. The once-crisp bacon has been softened by the thick, wet slice of tomato, and my mouth feels as though it is full of paste.

"Oh god," Candy mumbles around a mouthful, covering her mouth with her palm. "It's such a long story." She swallows hard, then continues. "Hunter was attacked by his ex-boyfriend last summer. He had a gun. Angus, you met him briefly the other day, was shot. Geoff—the ex—was sentenced to ten years in prison just a few weeks ago." She pops open the container of fruit and selects a wedge of pineapple.

"Is Angus Hunter's boyfriend?" I ask, thinking of the Alpha's arm around the cafe owner, his sharp teeth when he confronted me in the bathroom.

"Yeah," Candy replies. "Geoff found out about them and lost his shit."

"Do you like him?"

Candy holds the fruit container out to me, and I politely select a strawberry, its green tuft of leaves already sheared off. "He's nice," she replies. "He really cares about my brother and his grandma."

I nearly drop the strawberry. I plunge my fingers into its red flesh, juice trickling down my fingers. "He has a grandmother?"

Candy surveys me. "Yeah," she says slowly. "Ama Chilton."

I think of the woman in the dusty photographs, the way her curlicue handwriting carefully labelled each one. She wrote my grandfather's name with a little flourish on the 'm,' giving it a smile. "Candy," I say slowly, "I think that Ama is who I came to Wharton to find."

"Really?" Candy's face is bright, as though imbued with its own inner light. She's pleased. After all, she had wanted to help me — she is helping me. "You never explained why you were here."

"She knew my grandfather," I offer. "He died recently, and I want to know more about him." I lean back against the couch cushions, pulling my legs up against my chest.

"She lives out on Bird's Nest," Candy says, "but she doesn't come into town much. She's been sick, I think."

"Do you think you could introduce me?" For the moment, I don't think about the man found stashed under the bed, nor the fire that drove me here.

"Me?" Candy squeaks. "No. I've only met her once, and she yelled at me about the temperature of her latte. *But* Hunter knows her very well. Let me speak to him tomorrow. We're doing inventory together."

CHAPTER FOURTEEN
(CANDY)

◁◆▷

The dry storage area is like a tomb. I am surrounded by chrome-plated wire shelving on three sides, stacked high with dry goods, cleaning supplies, and silverware. It's dim and inordinately quiet. I have to use my phone light to read labels, scrunching my eyes until the words become clear.

A hand clasps my shoulder and I shout, whirling.

Hunter chuckles, a bottle of Ketel One in-hand. "Look what I found," he exclaims. It's covered in a fine layer of dust, the label faded and curling at the corners. "It was in the back of a cabinet, should we see if it's still good?" He doesn't wait for an answer, cranking the top until it gives way. He hands it to me. "Ladies first."

The smell is strong. I can nearly feel my nose hairs sizzling. Squeezing my eyes shut tight, I take a quick gulp. The alcohol sears its way down my esophagus, settling heavily in my belly. I wordlessly hand the bottle back.

Hunter takes a swallow, then another. He sputters, wiping the clear liquid off his chin. "Well, it hasn't gone bad," he finally says.

"It hasn't gone *good* either." I laugh. I skirt around him, reaching into the enormous commercial refrigerator for a carton of juice. "I'll mark it on the inventory sheet," I tell him, when his jaw tenses into a right angle. "Calm down." I pour two glasses of orange juice, then add a liberal splash of the vodka.

I lean against the basin sink. "We've been at this for hours," I complain. My neck aches, and there's a sore crescent just between my shoulder blades that I can't seem to stretch out. I roll my shoulders, dropping my chin to my chest, to no avail.

"Remember doing this as kids?" Hunter asks. "My fingers would lock up after folding t-shirts."

I remember. Our parents would let us stay up late on inventory days, and we would watch old movies on a shitty CRT monitor while we worked. Dad loved the Universal monsters. Back then, the store didn't sell food, and we would splurge on bags of family-sized chips from the grocery store. I remember getting fluorescent orange Cheeto dust on a white tee and getting in huge trouble for damaging merchandise. The shirt came out of that month's allowance.

There's a thud from upstairs, and it shakes the fluorescent light strip above our heads. "Is someone in the loft?" Hunter asks. His eyes grow round. "Is Julien back?"

"No," I reply. I take a drink, wincing. I put too much vodka in the mix, the pulpy juice can't subdue the liquor's fire. "Haley is actually staying with me."

"Good morning," Haley murmurs, from her nest on the couch. Her chin-length hair is a rat's nest atop her head. The sun, streaming through the blinds, makes the golden strands appear to smolder.

I startle. I didn't realize she was awake. I had been on my way to the bathroom, tiptoeing past the coffee table. "Oh!" I exclaim. "Shit! Sorry, I...good morning to you, too." I'm only wearing panties and a long tee, pilfered from Julien months ago. I feel naked. I tug at the hem, but it barely covers the tops of my thighs.

To her credit, Haley doesn't look. Her amber eyes remain on my face.

"You'll talk to Hunter today, right?" she asks. "About Ama?"

"Of course," I reply, shifting from foot to foot. The carpet squishes between my toes. "Tonight, at inventory. I'll be right back." I retreat to the bathroom, locking the door behind me. My heart patters in my chest. I try very hard not to think about how I wanted her to look at me. I wanted to watch her eyes course down my frame, for her lips to part just slightly when—

Stop.

I stare into the bathroom mirror, examining my sleep-creased cheek and the bit of acne on my chin. I can't stop thinking about the girl on my couch. Last night, I listened to the sound of her breathing, wishing she was lying beside me. I couldn't help thinking about the two of us sitting side-by-side on my couch, our hands and mouths slick with pineapple juice as we passed the flimsy container back and forth.

Oh, Candy, stop it.

When I open the bathroom door, she is right there. I nearly collide with her, and her fingertips rest on my hipbones, steadying me. "Hey," she says. She's dressed already, wearing cutoffs and a t-shirt with a tiny pocket over the breast. She has a pair of sunglasses dangling there. "I was just going to ask if you wanted to go to the beach before your shift," she continues. She releases me, but the ghost of her touch remains.

"I would love to," I whisper, hardly able to find my voice. "Let me get changed."

"Haley is staying with you?" Hunter asks. His expression is unreadable. I'm not entirely sure whether he's asking out of curiosity or concern.

"The Cove closed down," I explain. "She had nowhere else to go. I like her." I take another gulp, secretly glad when the alcohol wraps me in its warm embrace. Everything starts to feel floaty, pleasant. "I think I really like her."

"I'm not going in alone!" Haley squeals, grabbing my hand and pulling me toward the breakers. The foam laps against our toes. It's chilly, and I want to run in the opposite direction toward our towels. "Candy!" she wheedles, and I give in, letting her pull me into the surf.

We have to run or else we'll lose our nerve, the sand silky soft beneath the soles of our feet. When we are waist deep, we pause, laughing to keep from weeping. It's so cold—unbearably so—but there's no going back.

"I dare you to go under," Haley says as a wave laps against our bellies. Gooseflesh courses up my abdomen. My nipples tighten.

"You first."

Haley runs her wet hands through her hair. "Together," she concedes. She grabs my hand, and we both turn to face an incoming wave. "Ready?" she says. I nod, watching the wave roll, its lip curling. "Now!" she shouts, and we both dive, slipping under the trough. I kick off the sand, bursting out of the water with a gasp.

"That's so fucking cold," I shout, pushing my soaking bangs off my forehead with my free hand. She's still holding my hand, our fingers interlocked. My heart thumps, though I'm not sure if it's from the teeth-rattling cold or her touch.

"We're definitely going to get hypothermia," Haley agrees, but then she grins. "Let's do it again."

"You like her," Hunter repeats slowly. He is quiet for a long moment, forehead wrinkled as if he's solving a very complicated puzzle. "Candy, there's something you should know about—"

Something heavy slams against the exterior door, rattling it in its frame. We both jump, and my drink sloshes over the back of my hand, droplets raining onto the polished concrete floor. "What was *that*?" I hiss.

"I'm not sure," Hunter says, drifting toward the door. He rests his palms on the push bar. "Maybe there's a raccoon playing in the dumpster."

"That's a big fucking raccoon," I mutter. I want to tell Hunter not to open the door. It's locked from the inside, and as long as he doesn't depress the bar, no one can come in. I think, momentarily, of the dead man at The Cove, whose photo has dominated the airwaves all day. It's a shot of the blond man in a plush, green backyard, sitting on the slide of a Little Tykes playground. He's far too large: his butt at the apex, and his feet in the grass. A little girl with bouncy braids stands on the play structure just behind him, her arms slung around his neck.

Hunter eases the door open and leans into the alleyway. It's quite dark; the only illumination is a small motion-activated light above the door. It clicks when Hunter trips the sensor. "Nothing," he announces, stepping outside.

I step out after him, leaving the door ajar with a discarded cinderblock we kept for just that purpose. I look up and down the alley, at the hulking shapes of dumpsters placed equidistant from one another.

"That was weird," I mutter. "Let's get back to work. It's getting late."

Suddenly, something slams into my shoulder. Off-balance, I fall to the pavement, scraping my palms on the rough surface. Hunter screams, his back colliding with the dumpster. A metallic *clang* ripples through the air. *What's happening?*

A large *something* stands between Hunter and the safety of the cafe. It's enormous; if they stood toe-to-claw, Hunter's nose would brush against its sternum. Its face is somewhat wedge-shaped, ending in a tapered muzzle. I can just make out two rows of sharp, long teeth and a lolling tongue. I can't quite make sense of it. Is it a rabid dog, its misfiring nerve synapses causing it to stand upright? No, it's much too large, hundreds of pounds heavier than even the largest dog I've ever seen. Its coloring—dark charcoal, lighter daubs of silver across its muzzle—is more wolf-like than dog-like. *A wolf!*

I can't help but think of Hunter's ex-boyfriend Geoff sitting in my apartment, telling me Hunter was seeing things. Delusions.

Hunter wasn't—isn't—delusional.

The wolf pulls its lips away from its jaws in a gruesome amalgamation of a smile. "Nice to see you again, Hunter Bailey."

"Le...Leigh?" Hunter stammers. The wolf creeps closer. Hunter flattens against the stinking dumpster, turning his head away and squeezing his eyes shut. Tears trickle down his cheeks.

"Where's Angus?" the wolf asks, its voice a snarl.

"I don't know," Hunter manages, his lips quivering.

The wolf reaches out, curling its paw around Hunter's throat. "Call him," the wolf commands.

This must be a nightmare. Maybe I drank too much, sucking down decades-old vodka amidst the dry goods. *I fell asleep,* I soothe myself. *I'm sleeping, my head cushioned on a 500-count pack of napkins.*

But, if this is a dream, it's far more realistic than any I've ever had before. I can smell the wolf's fur, somewhat musky. If I were brave enough to stroke it, my hands would come away somewhat oily.

Hunter's mouth gapes. He can't breathe.

"Stop!" I scream. I pick up the hefty cement doorstop, and the door shuts with a pneumatic *fwuump*. With a labored grunt, I heave it at the wolf's head as though I'm throwing a shot-put. *Yip!* The brick grazes the wolf's muzzle, and it lurches backward. Whirling, the wolf knocks me onto my back, and my head strikes the ground. My vision blurs for a dizzying moment, and all I can think about is the kaleidoscope I had as a kid.

When my sight clears, I am looking up between the buildings and the night sky. There are no stars, just swollen, noctilucent clouds. I slowly sit up, my fingers splayed on the pavement; it's cool, a balm for my hurting body. The wolf's snout is bleeding, blood intermingling with thick globules of saliva. Her attention is back on Hunter, who is babbling now.

"Angus isn't here, okay?" Hunter says. "He left, went back to Portland, didn't even say goodbye."

"Liar," the wolf snickers. She grabs a fistful of his t-shirt, lifting him off his feet. The toes of his sneakers scrape against the pavement. "You know," she says, her voice a veritable purr. "I've really come to see what James saw in it—eating your kind, I mean. You're starting to smell really, really good, Hunter. Call him, please. I'm getting peckish."

Hunter relents, reaching into his pocket for his phone. But, before he can dial, the Ebb and Flow door swings open. The three of us squint in the bright, fluorescent light. Angus is standing there, a takeout container from Dottie's in his hand. Our eyes meet: me, sitting on the ground, and him, bathed in light like a saint in a Renaissance painting. Then, he sees the wolf, and Hunter dangling from her claw. "Leigh!" His voice is inordinately loud, drawing the beast's attention. "Put him down."

"I don't think I will," Leigh says. "I think I'll kill him while you watch."

Angus steps into the alley, and the door closes behind him. For a moment, it is very dark, and I can't see anything. The takeout container falls to the ground, its contents exploding wetly from it. *Pasta, I think.* Dottie makes an exceptional carbonara that Hunter adores. A sickening popping sound follows, reminding me of the time my shoulder dislocated after I tumbled roller-skating on the pier.

Something large passes by me, and fur brushes against my cheek. I recoil.

My eyes finally adjust as Angus collides with Leigh. Or, rather, what I imagine was once Angus. He's an enormous wolf-creature now, too, his fur bright white. Hunter is thrown from Leigh's grasp, landing heavily near the dumpster. I crawl toward him, kneeling in something foul-smelling and sticky. "Hunter? Are you okay?"

Hunter groans in response but nods.

The wolves tussle, their teeth flashing. They snarl in what becomes a gruesome melody, punctuated by yips and whines. I have a hard time looking at them. My eyes want to slide away, to focus on something comprehensible. The dark-colored wolf leaps away from its opponent, blood streaming from a deep laceration in its side. Its fur is matted and slick with blood.

"This isn't over," it gasps before turning tail and running from which it came. The big white wolf— Angus—doesn't follow.

CHAPTER FIFTEEN
(ANGUS)

—◁◆▷—

I slide three chairs off a cafe table, tucking them in so that Hunter and Candy can sit. Hunter sinks into one gratefully, but Candy paces the length of the room, shaking her head. Neither seem to realize I'm stark naked, and I excuse myself to the back room to pull a change of clothes out of Hunter's locker. I find a pair of sweatpants and pull them on, snickering when I discover that the cuff rests mid-calf. Hunter is much smaller than I am. I can't find a shirt, but his Ebb and Flow zip-up sweatshirt is draped over his office chair.

When I return to the cafe proper, Hunter has his face in his hands. Candy is red-faced, babbling, "What the absolute *fuck* is going on here? Did I hit my head at the beach, am I in a *coma?* Because that's the only thing that explains any of this."

I can't help but remember explaining wolfishness to Hunter. It was right here, in this very cafe. He kissed me after. But Candace Bailey is not her brother.

"Candy," I say whisper-soft. She jumps, whirling to face me. "I'm really sorry you found out like this."

"Geoff told me Hunter was crazy," she stammers. "I was calling psychiatrists, asking how to have him committed."

Geoff's name is like a kick to the stomach. I rest my hand on Hunter's shoulder, and he covers my hand with his, offering me a gentle pat. "Geoff knew what I was." I sigh. "And he tried to kill me. I'm sure you have a lot of questions."

"No." Candy laughs. "I don't because this *isn't happening*."

"Sit down, Candace." Hunter gestures to the chair beside his. His voice is hoarse. Candy stares at him, nibbling at her nails. "Please," he adds. With a sigh, she finally deigns to sit down. As Hunter starts to patiently tell his sister about the world he inadvertently stumbled upon when we met, I move closer to the picture window, peering out onto Main Street. It's just past midnight now, and most of the businesses are shuttered for the night. A few pedestrians walk the streets.

A person in a baseball cap pauses outside of Ebb and Flow, lighting a cigarette. He has the same wide, broad build as James had, and for a moment, I think I've seen a ghost. But, when the zippo ignites, I catch a glimpse of ginger hair and eyes the color of garnet. I'm mistaken.

James is dead, I remind myself.

But Leigh is very much alive, and she's here in Wharton. *I think I'll kill him while you watch*, she'd said gleefully.

I press my forehead against the cool windowpane, closing my eyes. That's not the Leigh I remember. But she'd lost her brother—her twin. With a pang, I think of the way they would speak over one another, finishing each other's sentences. I wonder if Leigh catches herself waiting for him to speak, the words perched on the tip of her tongue.

"Angus." Candy rests her elbow on the back of her chair, surveying me. "You're bleeding." She points at her own forehead, drawing a line from hairline to temple. Gingerly, I touch my forehead, examining my bloody fingers. Hunter grabs a handful of napkins from the dispenser and comes to press them against my head. I offer him a tight smile of thanks.

"I need to go to bed," Candy says. "Maybe if I sleep, all of *this* will make sense."

Hunter gives his sister a one-armed squeeze, keeping his other hand on my bleeding face. "I'll lock up," he assures her. "Call me tomorrow, okay?"

"Yeah," she murmurs.

As she walks into the backroom, taking the stairwell up, I turn my attention to my lover. His eyebrows are knitted together in concern, the very tip of his tongue peeking between his lips as he concentrates.

"I'm okay, love," I assure him.

"You need stitches," Hunter says, pulling the napkins away just enough to get a good look. "It's deep."

I'm not concerned about my wound. I tilt his chin just slightly, so I can see his throat. There's some petechiae, red blooms crawling up the sides of his neck, and a faint purplish bruise just above his Adam's apple. "Are you okay?" I ask.

"Fine," Hunter says shortly. "It hurts to talk. What are we going to do about Leigh?"

"We're going home, and we're getting the pack together. I'm going to find her and settle this." I don't elaborate further. Instead, I allow the plan to settle, half-formed, like a cardigan around Hunter's shoulders. It is enough to comfort him, to smooth out the worry lines in his forehead.

"There," Renner grunts, snipping away the remainder of thread with a pair of kitchen shears. He leans back on the ottoman, examining his handiwork from a distance, then seemingly satisfied, takes a swig from the bottle of whiskey sitting at his feet. "Just as easy to fix as a torn spinnaker," he remarks.

"Thanks, Ren." I grin. "Hopefully, I'll look as pretty as one, too."

"Ayuh." He doesn't sound entirely convinced. Renner is tall and lanky, his ribs jutting out beyond his suspenders. Sitting on the ottoman, he appears to be folded in half, his knees nearly touching his chest.

He was quick to come when Hunter beckoned him, emerging from his houseboat with a small, red medic bag and a bottle of whiskey. He's dressed in a pair of woolen Long Johns, held up with suspenders, and a dirty, white tank top. The whiskey bottle was already half-empty, and the woodsy aroma of it seemed to seep from his pores. "Liquid courage," he'd explained, handing it to me, but it was apparent he and the bottle had been spending much of the night together. Still, his hands were steady, and unlike the Emergency Room, he didn't ask invasive questions.

Renner scratches at his pigeon chest with dirty nails. "Should I take a little jog up Bird's Nest, make sure there aren't any she-wolves sniffing around your granny's place?"

"Alexandre is there," I assure him. "I called him on the way home." I look over at Hunter, who is dozing on the couch. He's sitting up, his chin resting heavily in his palm. "It's late," I continue. "Let's all be as alert as we can tonight, then meet up in the morning here."

"Ayuh," Renner agrees. He rises, tucking the whiskey bottle under his arm. "Get some rest. and get that one to bed. I'll stay up and have a little campout on the quarter deck. I'll be able to see your place from there, a bit of the street too."

"I appreciate that." I'm secretly glad for the offer. Now that the adrenaline has dissipated, I'm dog-tired.

Renner steps out on the back deck and down into the sand. It's only a few yards to the dock, his house-boat bobbing. I keep the deck light on until he climbs the boat's ladder, throwing his leg over the side. It's an ugly, square-shaped vessel, rusty red with a smattering of barnacles on the hull. I've been inside once or twice. It reeked of unwashed bodies and tuna, and the rooms were so compact I had to bend over to walk through the doorways.

Before I close and lock the door, Renner flips on the large spotlight mounted on the boat. The circle of light slides up the sand, then points directly at our bungalow, hurting my eyes. The spotlight clicks off, relighting again some distance away. *Go to bed*, Renner says without saying anything at all. *I'm watching*.

I kiss Hunter's bowed head. "Let's go to bed," I murmur, rousing him with a gentle shake. With his eyes half-lidded, he allows me to lead him to the bedroom. Before he can fall upon the mattress, I unbutton his jeans, letting them pool around his ankles. He steps out of them, yawning as I pull his shirt up over his head. I can't help but to kiss his chest, smack dab in the constellation of freckles there. His wiry chest hair tickles my lips.

"Mmm," he murmurs.

"Goodnight, Hunt," I tell him, kissing his cheek, then the very corner of his sleepy half-smile. "I'll be back in a minute."

While he burrows under the bedsheets, I step into the bathroom, flipping on the light. I peer into the mirror at my face, examining the stitches Renner had done. There are a dozen in all, placed somewhat haphazardly, the thread stained dark with blood.

I sigh. It's just another scar left by the Volkov siblings, another reminder of the mistake I made letting James leave Portland. I run my hands through my beard, feeling the slightly raised, thin cicatrices left by James' claws on my cheeks. *Just another scar.*

CHAPTER SIXTEEN
(CANDY)

———◁◆▷———

Haley is dozing on the couch, wearing my wireless Bose headphones. When I lean close, I can hear the dulcet melody of what I think is a Petals for Armor song. Haley lays with her arm thrown over her head, her nose tucked into the crook of her elbow. Her short hair encircles her head like a halo.

I feel as though I'm drunk—or maybe, I *am* drunk. I can still taste the acidic orange juice on my tongue from my mixed drink. Did I finish the cup before the wolf came? Maybe I could find the neglected cup if I lean out onto the fire escape. Surely, with a bird's eye view, I could find it, upturned on the grimy asphalt. I don't dare move toward the window. I'm afraid if I look, I'll see some*thing* looking back.

Haley murmurs in her sleep, the words indecipherable. They may not have even been words at all. Perhaps it was an incantation, spoken in an arcane tongue. I sit on the edge of the couch. My hand hovers above her shoulder. I don't want to be alone. I don't want to think about the wolf that threatened my brother's life, nor the wolf that shares his bed.

"Haley?" I whisper, touching her arm.

Haley's eyelids crinkle, and her lips purse. But she doesn't wake, not entirely. I gently take the headphones off her head, placing them on the coffee table. I can hear the singer's soprano voice through the speakers.

"Haley?" I say again.

Her amber eyes crack open. "Candy?" she manages, stifling a yawn with the back of her hand. "What time is it?" She glances around the room, as if surprised to find it dark, thick with shadow.

"Late," I reply. "I'm really sorry to wake you, I just—" I'm not sure what to say.

Haley props herself up on her elbows. "Are you okay?"

I shake my head, irritated at the hot tears threatening to spill forth. *Don't cry*, I admonish myself. "I don't know," I finally whisper, afraid my voice will betray the turbulence inside me. I wish I could forget the image of my brother's red face, his eyes bulging as the wolf squeezed his windpipe. I wish I could forget the wolf and her husky voice, speaking not in growls but in words I could understand. It felt paradoxical, incongruous. I feel much like Alice in Wonderland did when she shrunk to the size of a dormouse. Even the Queen of Hearts would have difficulty believing this quite impossible thing.

A single, errant tear escapes, and Haley brushes it away with her finger. "You can talk to me," she assures me, "if you want to."

I suddenly find myself thinking of Juliette DeMarco. She had the same look in her eyes just before I kissed her. She was the first and only girl.

Juliette DeMarco's dorm room is smaller than mine: a single, rather than a double. The painted cinderblock walls are bare, save for a flock of Polaroids taped above her desk. I lean close to examine them: a gaggle of cheerleaders perched on the bleachers, Juliette sticking out her tongue in their midst; a dog with a tennis ball in its slobbery mouth; a family portrait, taken in front of a Christmas tree; and Juliette in her Halloween costume, dressed like Gwen Stefani in the Sweet Escape music video. The striped pants make her legs appear inordinately long.

"Don't look at those," Juliette groans. "They're embarrassing."

"You're the one who put them up," I observe coolly.

"I didn't expect guests." Juliette sits on her small bed, crossing her legs. She's wearing cutoff shorts, and the fabric rides up her thighs.

I try not to stare. I've had a crush on her since freshmen orientation, or rather, what Hunter calls a crush.

I don't know whether you want to be her or fuck her, *Hunter laughs.*

"You're lucky. I don't get a moment of peace with Dina," I remark, referring to my roommate. She's always on the phone with her long-distance boyfriend, exchanging I love yous and no, you hang up firsts.

Juliette's desk is pristine, everything in its place. I pick up a Hello Kitty pencil holder, giving it a shake.

The writing implements inside the feline's enormous plastic head rattle. One of the pencils has been chewed, squarish indentations ringing the eraser. I didn't take Juliette to be the pencil chewing type. It almost makes her seem human, rather than the perfect automaton I know her as. I put the pencil holder back where I found it.

It's Saturday afternoon, and outside, underclassmen play in the grassy courtyard. Shouts and laughter trickle through the cracked window, escorted by a cool breeze. It ruffles Juliette's chestnut hair.

"Did you have a chance to type up the bibliography?" Juliette asks, eager to get on with it. She really doesn't like me in her room.

"Yeah." I sit on her bed beside her. I reach into my backpack, pulling out my battered Dell laptop. It's seen better days; there's a dent in the case, and many of the stickers I'd decorated it with have turned pearly and gritty due to accidental water exposure.

Juliette wrinkles her nose. I wake the computer with a key press. When the screen illuminates, Juliette scoots closer so she can see. Her thigh presses firmly against mine.

The wallpaper is a photo of me and my boyfriend, Wes. He's still home in Wharton, working on his father's crabbing boat. I've been avoiding his calls, dreading another diatribe about the choppy seas, how hauling traps has really enhanced his biceps. But, most of all, I don't want to have to say, "I love you, too."

It feels like a lie. It is a lie, because at night, I'm really thinking about Juliette DeMarco.

"Are you sure you have enough?" Juliette asks.

"Professor Ackerman asked for five sources. There's five." Annoyance courses through my muscles, gumming them up like lactic acid. My shoulders tighten around my ears.

"But is it enough*?"* Juliette gives me a sidelong look. *"Just because that's the minimum doesn't mean our research is done."* Up close, her hazel eyes are ringed with prehnite green. I am reminded, suddenly, of the creeper vines crawling up the back fence at my parent's house, coiling tightly around the chicken wire. I feel a bit choked myself.

"It's enough," I insist. *"Or would you rather do it yourself?"*

"What about the tables?" Juliette asks, not bothering to disguise the exasperation in her voice. *"Did you do them?"*

I suck at my teeth. *"Not yet,"* I reply. *"I figured we would do them together—it'll be faster if you read me the measurements."* In truth, I had simply forgotten. I reach into my bag for my spiral-bound notebook, passing it to her. It's dog-eared, the front cover sheared off.

Juliette hesitates, but opens it, using only the very tips of her fingers as though it's soiled. *"Okay, are you ready?"* she asks, when she finds the page labeled *Titration of a Diprotic Acid.* When I answer in the affirmative, she reads off various PH balances and the analogous titrant drop volume. Her voice is soft, and I have to lean toward her in order to hear. I can feel the heat of her breath on my skin.

"Hold on," I say, midway through, my fingers cramping. I reach into my bag again, pulling out

two tall cans of Four Loko from the six-pack stashed therein. I press one, still cool, into her hand.

"It's not even three o'clock," Juliette protests, holding the can limply between her knees. I pop the top on mine, taking a swig. It's sour apple, and my lips pucker involuntarily. Juliette snickers at me, as though I've gotten what I deserved.

"We're in for a long night. We may as well have fun, DeMarco. Drink up." I reach over and pop the top on her yet-unopened can. She raises it to her lips and takes a sip. I was kind and gave her the strawberry lemonade flavor.

Juliette rolls her eyes. "Start typing, Candace."

Twenty minutes later, I push my laptop aside, laying back on Juliette's bedspread. It's well past sunset, and we have been working by the pale yellow light of her desk lamp. The light makes us both look a bit jaundiced and has given me a bit of a headache. Or is it the Four Loko? The alcohol sloshes in my belly. We've had two cans each. The empties sit on the desk in a staggered row. "I'm starving," I complain.

"We're nearly done," Juliette reminds me. "But there's a vending machine down the hall." She grabs my hand, hauling me to my feet. I nearly stumble into her, and we giggle. The alcohol has turned Juliette's cheeks pink, upturned the corners of her mouth.

The vending machine hums in a small alcove. Juliette swipes her Captains Card, inputting the code A-3. The metal spirals in that row turn, releasing a package of mini powdered donuts. She swipes again, looking at me expectantly. "What do you want? My treat."

"*Doritos,*" *I reply.* "*Cool Ranch.*"

Juliette types D-6, retrieving the chips from the dispenser. She tosses them to me. I fumble, dropping them. We both titter.

Back in the room, Juliette closes the window. It's chilly now, the sun having taken all its heat with it to the other hemisphere. She sits cross-legged on the bed, picking open the corners of the donut's plastic wrap. Carefully, she pops a whole donut in her mouth. The white powder clings to her upper lip, and she swipes it away with her tongue. "*God, I love these,*" *she groans, her mouth full.*

I suddenly feel shy. I perch on the edge of her bed, crinkling the bag in my hands. We aren't just working on an assignment anymore. We're hanging out like friends, *or maybe, something more than that.* "*I'm not really into sweets,*" *I mumble.* "*They give you cavities.*" *It's not exactly true. I'm not sure why I'm lying.*

Juliette reaches into the package for another donut. "*Maybe that's why I'm prone to cavities.*"

My stomach churns. In the meager light of the desk lamp, I am suddenly very aware of the knife-sharp edge of her jaw. When she smiles, dimples poke hollows into her cheeks. I wonder then, what it would be like to kiss her there. My face grows hot.

I reach into my backpack for the last two cans of Four Loko. I offer her the other, but she shakes her head.

I take three big gulps. It's peach-flavored, and the tartness settles heavily on my tongue. The alcohol wraps my brain in a thin layer of cotton. Juliette is suddenly on her knees beside me, a donut in hand. "*You have to try one,*" *she wheedles.* "*Just a little bite.*"

She presses the donut against my lips, and I take a tentative bite. There's a surreal chilliness as the powdered sugar dissolves in my hot mouth, and the cake beneath is airy and soft, albeit slightly stale. It tastes bland but with a hint of vanilla. "It tastes like it has been in the vending machine for one hundred years." I laugh.

Juliette laughs. "You just have no taste." She eats the rest of the donut, a smear of powdered sugar glazing her lips. Without thinking, I brush it away with my thumb. She stares at me, lips parted. "Candy—"

Is it an invitation or a warning?

She leans close, her breath warming my face. Suddenly emboldened, I traverse the short divide between us, pressing my lips against hers. The alcohol is my armor. Tentative, I touch her cheek with my shaking fingers, tracing the line of her jaw. When her hand touches my breast, though, I jerk backward, nearly falling off the narrow bed onto the floor. "I've got to go," I mumble, "I can't—"

I wanted to kiss her. I desperately wanted to. But her touch frightened me because it meant she wanted to kiss me, too. It felt dangerous, like putting my hand into a crocodile's mouth.

Juliette frowns. "I thought—"

"I'm sorry," I manage, shouldering my bag. The remaining can of Four Loko bumps painfully against my hip. "I'm really sorry." I leave my laptop behind. When Juliette returns it during our next class, lingering next to my chair, I can't quite meet her eyes.

"It's been a long night," I finally say. "I shouldn't have woken you up. I just didn't want to be alone."

Haley sits up, and suddenly, we are inches apart. My impulse is to stand, to step away so the coffee table is an island between us. But I'm so, so tired. I'm tired of fighting, I'm tired of the adrenaline making me turn tail and run. It's not lost on me that I didn't run from the wolf in the alleyway. Instead, I crept toward her, desperate to check on my ailing brother, his neck ringed in purple.

Tentative, I touch Haley's hair, the silken strands sliding between my thumb and forefinger. Her hair is thick, lustrous, the color of wild things. Then, I curl my hand around the nape of her neck, cupping the knotted vertebrae there. Haley's fingertips brush against my knee, feather-light, inching up the bunched muscle in my thigh. When I pull her close, her lips part slightly, her breath hot on my face. "Can I kiss you?" I whisper.

"Please," she breathes, then her lips are on mine. Heat pools between my legs as her tongue gently presses into my mouth, sliding wetly against mine. Haley's palm rests firmly on my thigh now, her fingertips dimpling my flesh. Our teeth clack together, and we pull apart, laughing. Haley's eyes are the color of warm honey, and when she laughs, they seem to ignite with inner light.

I expect for the spell to be broken. I expect for my hammering heart to force me to get up and leave. But I'm still cradling her neck, and her hand is still on my thigh. I press my lips to hers again, and she mewls into my mouth as though she's longed for this. I want to tell her I did too. Her hand crawls up my thigh, her fingertips resting just beneath the hem of my jean shorts. *God*.

Haley's kisses pepper my jaw, the hollow of my neck. She sucks the sensitive flesh there between her teeth, and I am shocked by the moan seeping from my mouth. Her hair smells tropical, like mango; she's used my shampoo. Something about that is incredibly intimate, titillating.

Haley pauses, her breath hot on my neck. "We can stop," she murmurs, "if you want." Her hand on my thigh flexes.

I'm embarrassed by my own panting. I shift my thigh just slightly, and her fingers slip a bit more beneath the denim. I don't want to stop. I realize Haley is panting too. The very tip of her tongue draws a languid circle on my neck. I wonder what I taste like. I wonder what *she* tastes like. "I don't want to stop," I finally say, knowing I am standing on the edge of a precipice. Or have I already jumped off?

Haley's hand leaves my thigh, and I whimper in disappointment. But she reaches for the button of my shorts, urging me to rise as she slides them down my thighs. Even in the dark room, I feel exposed in only my panties and t-shirt. Gooseflesh trickles up my thighs. "You're shaking," Haley observes, looking up at me.

"I've never done this before," I admit.

Haley cups the back of my thighs, pulling me down onto her lap. Her hands slip beneath my shirt, gliding up my belly. "I'll go slow," she assures me. "You tell me what you need." She cups my breasts through my bra, the pads of her thumbs rousing my nipples beneath the thin fabric.

She kisses my mouth, letting my tongue probe between her lips. As we kiss, she unclasps my bra with practiced hands, pushing the cups off my breasts. When she touches me again, I am struck by the heat of her palms. After caressing me for a moment, she pulls my shirt and the dangling bra off, then tosses them aside. "Beautiful," she groans, her teeth snagging my lip. Her hands return to my thighs, sliding purposefully up to the hemline of my panties.

Her thumb slides across the gusset of my panties, barely touching me. My thighs spasm. *Please,* I want to say, but I needn't ask. Haley already knows. She slips her hand between the fabric and my skin, finding the pink nub that causes the muscles in my core to tighten. I find myself grinding my hips against her hand, wanting more, *more, MORE.*

It feels altogether different from Julien's touch. He would rub me there with the heel of his hand, but not for more than a moment. He wanted to be inside of me, wanted to watch his cock slide in and out of my folds. Haley sucks my nipple into her mouth, and an unexpected orgasm causes my body to quake. I throw my arms around Haley's swanlike neck, my body pressing tight against hers. When I finally settle, panting, she is nearly thrumming with kinetic energy, as if I am a live wire.

"Candy," she murmurs, burying her face between my breasts. "I need to go."

"What?" I am desperate to touch her, wanting to make her feel good, but she grasps my hands.

"I can't explain," she gasps. "Not right now. But I can't stay here, in this apartment, with you."

"Why?" She gently pushes me off her lap, and I pull my legs up to my chest. I feel embarrassed, and I don't want her looking at my naked body anymore. "Did I do something wrong?" My voice sounds plinky, like a broken piano key.

She leans over, pressing her lips against my forehead. "I'm sorry," she says, then she's gone, her feet loud and fast on the steps outside.

CHAPTER SEVENTEEN
(LEIGH)

———◁◆▷———

The spotlight sweeps across the line of bungalows, pouring white light through their windows. If it's keeping any of the residents awake, no one comes out to complain. Perhaps they are frightened of the volatile houseboat captain. I can hear him cursing to himself as he drops a bottle, glass skittering across the deck. The oaky smell of whiskey briefly fills my nose before the sea air sweeps it away.

A shame. I would have liked to try it.

It was easy to creep onto the houseboat undetected. The lapping of waves against the hull quieted my ascent up the ladder, and I found a hiding place in a small berth that had clearly been delegated for storage. I wedge myself amidst musty towels, coolers, a fan with only one blade, and what I suspect is a small, deflated dinghy.

Curious, I open the nearest cooler, and a crab, still very much alive, skitters out. It quickly disappears amongst the detritus, leaving behind tiny four-by-four tracks in the thick dust. The small window in the berth offers an obstructed view of the deck, the spotlight, and the captain's folding chair. I can see his bald head as he prowls around, grumbling to himself. I can't quite make out the words, but he talks incessantly, the words peppered with colorful curses.

Angus' newfound pack is pathetic, consisting of geriatrics and ne'er-do-wells. I passed Ama's bungalow an hour ago, finding it under the guard of an ancient, gaunt wolf. His eyes looked opaque in the porchlight, encased in cataracts. From my vantage point on the sand dunes, I watched him pant and pace. He was slow-going, barely able to hold his head up. Killing him would be a kindness, akin to euthanasia.

It had been strange to be near Ama's bungalow again. It looked much the same as I remembered, as if I'd just left for the afternoon. Even the lawn flamingo still leans heavily on its post, its curved beak plunging into the stagnant puddle beneath the gutter's down-spout. The only difference is a planter of butter-colored marigolds beside the porch rail, a new awning strung above the porch.

Luka shoulders open the bungalow's back door, ducking to wedge his enormous wolfish body through the doorframe. His fur snags in the hinges, leaving tangles of ebony pelage behind, but he doesn't complain; he may not even notice. James' head clunks heavily against the doorjamb, and I say, "careful!" before I remember that he can't feel it.

We shuffle into the cluttered living room, and Luka places James' body on the folded-out couch. "We need to pack," Luka says, trying to sound authoritative, brave, far older than his nineteen years. But his voice wobbles, thick with fettered emotion.

Conversely, tears and snot stream down my cheeks. I don't bother to wipe it away, and it becomes a second skin, making my face feel stiff.

Luka shrugs off his fur, his face scrunched in pain. "C'mon Leigh," he prompts when he discovers I still haven't moved. "We have to go now.*" His desire for haste is laughable. Angus is dying, each heartbeat pouring more of his blood onto the linoleum in Ebb and Flow. He'll probably die before the ambulance pulls up to the curb.*

I hope he dies.

It's a wicked thought, dreadful. One I've truly never had before. But it is like a balm for my grief, giving me just enough space in my chest cavity to take a full breath. Hunter's misery may cancel out mine. God, I hope he dies. I hope it hurts. I hope—

Ama Chilton shuffles out of her bedroom, big, fuzzy house slippers adorning her narrow feet. She looks down at James' body, her expression tranquil; she may as well be selecting a side of beef at the grocery store. "He couldn't help himself, could he?" she murmurs.

"Angus killed *him," I spit.*

Ama doesn't reply. She sits primly on the edge of the mattress, crossing one spindly ankle behind the other. She reaches toward my brother's face, closing his eyelids with two gnarled fingers. They only stay closed for a moment before easing open again. Now half-lidded, he looks just as he did when he was hungover, groaning over a plate of runny eggs at Lugano

Cafe. I can almost hear him say, Shouldn't have had that last Jaeger Bomb, Leigh. What a bad fucking idea.

"He did this to himself," Ama finally says. "He was supposed to leave town. He was supposed to let you two be free. But now, look what he's done!" She flaps her hands, nostrils flaring.

Luka leaves the two of us in the living room, ducking his head to avoid the old matriarch's eyes. Ama continues her diatribe, "This was senseless, and he dragged you two into this mess with him."

"He was my brother," I snarl.

Ama turns her attention to me. "He almost let you be happy, didn't he? But now, what will you do?"

Happiness is beyond my scope of understanding. I am like a carriage horse in blinders, only able to tramp forward. Whatever has happened before is covered in impenetrable fog. How could I ever be happy, sunning on the beach when the sun was covered in clouds?

Luka returns with an overstuffed bag, a sheen of sweat glistening on his forehead and upper lip. His eyes are red; he was crying in private, just a short blubber. "I think we're going south," he tells Ama, having overheard her question. "N'orleans, maybe. There are a lot of wolves there, or so they say."

Ama rises, clasping the younger man's hands. "You don't deserve this, son," she murmurs. "I am sorry he got his claws into you."

James's claws.

Before she can turn her attention to me, I slip into my pelt, into the fur that is so much like my brother's and grab the bag from Luka, slinging it over my narrow shoulder. "Let's go," I growl. "The sun will be up soon."

Luka nods reluctantly, offering Ama a final wan smile.

As fur sprouts on his face and chest, Ama gives me a final look. Her eyes are akin to scrying pools, I fear she can see everything I'm feeling. "He didn't let you go, but you can still be free. Don't let him poison you, sweet girl," she offers, solemn.

I didn't approach the house. Instead, I continued down the beach toward Hunter's bungalow. There, I found the houseboat and its spotlight.

The old captain is singing now, tapping his heel. The rhythmic sound fills the berth, rattling the thin walls. I almost feel as though I'm in the womb. "When I was a lil' boy my mother always told me," he warbles, "that if I din' kiss the girls, m'lip would grow all moldy."

I press my hand against my side, just beneath the curve of my rib. Angus' claws left behind a deep gash, and it hurts to move. It certainly hurts too much to be wolfish. Still, I have work to do. Angus can't wake up tomorrow feeling as though he's won.

I paw through more of the captain's things until I find a knife. It's meant for deboning fish; it has a narrow blade and a sharp point. There's also a reel of fishing line that seems strong enough to use as a garrote. *Marvelous.*

When the captain starts his second verse ("King Louis was the king of France before the Revolution…"), I step back out onto the deck. I slip the knife into my waistband and loop the line around my hands as though I'm preparing to play a game of cat's cradle.

When the captain raises his chin to sing a high note, I arc the line over his head, tightening it just beneath his jawline. He tries to leap to his feet, but he only succeeds in choking himself and upending his chair. He's strong, and I have to grit my teeth, pull my elbows tightly against my sides, let the scabbing wound tear open anew. He reaches back, clawing at my face with quickly lengthening nails, and I release the garrote.

The captain doubles over, coughing, pulling the razor-sharp wire out of the folds of his neck. But he never sits back up, because I slip the knife between two knobby vertebrae, severing the spinal cord.

Before I go, I turn off the spotlight. *Lights out.*

CHAPTER EIGHTEEN
(HALEY)

———◁◆▷———

It's nearly three o'clock in the morning; the pier is quiet. Even the carnival equipment is still, the Ferris wheel creaking when the wind hits the spokes just right. I lean against the rail, staring down at the dark, writhing water. It smells sulfurous, as though just beneath the waves is the gateway to hell. I stand on my tiptoes, resting my belly on the top rail. If I tip forward just slightly, I'll fall in.

I press my lips against the paper-thin flesh of Candy's sternum. The smell of her sweat—her arousal— fills my nostrils, musky and faintly saccharine. I long to drag my tongue up to her throat, nuzzle the supra-sternal notch between her clavicle, test the flesh there with my teeth. I would be gentle, so, so gentle to not pierce her jugular. But what if I wasn't?

Candy rests her cheek on the crown of my head, her breath a sigh. She shifts her weight, her hips pressing firmly against mine. A whit of pleasure heats my core,

*but suddenly, it feels markedly dangerous. It's a spark
that could ignite a fire, and the blaze will undoubtedly
consume everything it touches. I will lay waste to the
valleys and mountains of her.*

I've been caught playing with matches.

*"Candy, I need to go," I murmur, my voice muf-
fled between the curve of her breasts. When she leans
back, eyebrows knitted together, I want to take it back.
I wanted to make her feel good, to ease the worry lines
in her brow, but I've only succeeded in deepening them.*

*"What?" She tries to touch me, mimicking my own
ministrations mere moments ago, but I hold her hands
in mine. I can't bear it. If she touches me, I fear I won't
be tender, that the hunger will replace my arousal. I'm
having trouble discerning one impulse from the other.
"I can't explain," I hear myself saying. "Not right now.
But I can't stay here, in this apartment, with you."*

*I push her off my lap and stand. Her freckled arms
are wrapped tightly around her legs, her eyes downcast. She doesn't understand. Of course she doesn't.
How could she?*

*I lean close, kissing her head. "I'm sorry," I apol-
ogize; it's the least I can do. It sounds hollow. When I
grasp the doorknob, I find my fingers are gnarled, my
nails thick and yellowy. A spiral of silvery fur adorns
the back of my hand, and I can't help but think of a
labyrinth from which I can't escape.*

I am my own Minotaur.

I lean a little further, just enough to make myself
feel off-balance. I wonder what it would feel like if I
were to fall. The water is so dark it looks like oil. Is

the water as still as it seems, or would a current grasp me around the ankles, throwing me against the pier's thick, algae-slick pylons? Would the wolf attempt to fight for her life, even if my humanity closed her eyes?

The more I fight this inner battle, the more I see the wolf as an entirely separate being. She was the one who attacked Tara. She was the one who has perverted my every thought. She was the one who whispers into my ear, filling my head with intrusive thoughts.

Jump in.

I step away from the rail, skittering down the pier. The impulse frightens me, albeit not as much as my insistent hunger. I head down the steps, pausing on the penultimate step to remove my sneakers. The sand is still somewhat warm beneath my naked feet, and I dig my toes in.

I should return to Candy's apartment and apologize for running off, but I'm not quite ready yet. It's nearly morning—I can just see the faintest glimmer on the horizon line. If I dawdle, she might be asleep when I return, which is for the best; I'm not entirely sure what to say to her.

The beach on the north side of Wharton is wild, sea grass shimmering on the flanks of tall dunes. Boats bob beside narrow docks, thick braided ropes keeping them in place. I pass a crabbing vessel, wooden cages stacked along its center aisle. Then, several empty docks later, I walk abreast of a dilapidated houseboat.

"H-help," a small voice calls out. At first, I think it's a seagull, calling for its mate. But it calls again, "Please."

I pause, turning in a slow circle. *Where is it coming from?* My ears and nose are quite keen, even in this form, but the smell of the marina and the sound of water lapping against the boat's hull confuses my senses. I don't see anyone on the beach, nor on any of the narrow docks. I lean over, peering into the water, but can only see my wavering reflection. "Hello?" I say, feeling foolish.

Something raps against metal above my head: *tap, tap, tap... tap!* It's coming from somewhere on the houseboat. "Do you need help?" I call uneasily.

Tap, tap, taptaptap!

I approach the aft side of the boat, finding a metal ladder. Cautiously, I start to climb, my naked feet slipping on the wet surface. By the time I throw my legs over the side, the horizon is a swath of pink, offering a bit more light to see better. The boat bucks beneath my feet as I walk, and it makes me flounder, no nimbler than a newborn foal trying out its long, slender limbs for the first time.

The tapping continues with earnest, and I follow the sound toward the bow of the ship.

I nearly step on him. A man lays on the deck, his cheek resting in a pool of dark liquid. He taps his knuckle against the deck intermittently, an enormous pewter ring striking the fiberglass. *Tap, tap, tap!* Even though he's been discovered, he continues his unintelligible Morse code; I wonder if he even knows I'm here. The smell of alloy permeates the air here, and I know the dark liquid is blood.

I pull my phone out of my pocket, tapping the button to turn on the flashlight. The battery is nearly dead, the indicator stating two percent. *Shit*. With the meager, shaking beam, I can see he has been grievously injured. His face reminds me of a rubber Halloween mask. The blood loss is significant. His flesh is a dingy grey, and his lips are so pale they are indistinguishable from the rest of his facade; his mouth is just an empty, gasping hole. His eyes are wide, unblinking, the dark pupils usurping the irises.

"Help," he utters, the same voice I heard dockside.

I kneel beside him, searching for the source of the bleeding. I hold my phone in one hand, running my free one over his scalp, his ears, down his neck. Then, I find it: a knife handle sticking out of the back of his neck. "Jesus," I breathe. The stuck blade is keeping him alive; while blood leaks around the hilt, it's slow-moving.

The smell of blood makes me feel heady. I rise, blood soaking my naked legs and the hem of my shorts. I tap my phone screen, type 9-1–

The phone screen goes black, and I'm plunged back into darkness as the flashlight clicks off. "I'm going for help," I tell the man. "I'll be right back, okay?"

He doesn't answer, save for a plaintive *tap*.

I go back the way I came, finding the ladder and nearly sliding down to the dock below. I run toward the line of bungalows several hundred yards away, mounting the back deck of the nearest. I slap my hands against the sliding glass door, screaming. "Help! Help! Someone is in trouble!"

It's dark inside. But, with the sun rising at my back, I can just make out a couch, a coffee table, an enormous, leafy Monstera plant. A light clicks on, and a sliver of light lances out of the bottom of a closed door. Someone has heard me. "Help!" I scream again, shaking the door handle. The inner door opens, and a tall figure approaches. It pauses, a hand hovering over the sliding door's handle before throwing it open.

"Haley?" A bearded man says, looking down at me with sleepy eyes. He's wearing a silken kimono, a thick tuft of chest hair poking out of his deep V-shaped collar. The smell of petrichor fills my nostrils.

Angus Chilton.

CHAPTER NINETEEN
(ANGUS)

———————⊲◆⊳———————

The dock is crisscrossed with fluorescent yellow police tape, demarcating the marina from the floating crime scene. It's grown quiet in the last hour. The ambulance is long gone, and thankfully, we are no longer subjected to its keening. I fear the sound—the echo of it, its plaintive ghost—will never truly leave my ear canals. Only a few police officers remain, climbing all over the boat like a colony of ants.

From my vantage point on the back deck, I see camera flashes lighting up the bulkhead. Haley Campbell sits on the floorboards, her legs pretzeled beneath her, watching them work. Hunter brought her a warm washcloth to clean the blood off her skin, but she just holds it in her hands, squeezing droplets onto the wood.

"You saved his life," I remind her. It's not the first time I've said it. The police and paramedics said it too. There's a 'thank you' implicit therein.

Her shoulders rise up around her earlobes, then fall. *She's in shock*, I think. When I followed her to the boat, I was appalled by what I saw. I can't quite get Renner's eyes out of my head. When I touched his skin, called his name, he seemed to look through me. It was like I didn't exist at all. Surely, seeing him in the pewter light of daybreak was its own nightmare.

"Hunter is making coffee," I tell the younger woman. Through the sliding glass door, I see him in the kitchen, a trio of mugs parked on the countertop. In his haste to dress, he had put on one of my shirts. It's much too large for him, and the sleeves flare around his slender, ropy arms. It's an OMSI shirt, a minimalist screen print of the famous Portland science museum on the chest.

"I'm not thirsty," Haley murmurs.

"Your last name is Campbell, isn't it?" I ask, thinking of the photo album Ama showed me a few days ago. Haley looks up at me, raising her eyebrows. She certainly has the same eyes as the man in the photograph: striking, dark, evasive.

"Yes," she replies.

"I spoke to my grandmother about you after you mentioned my grandfather, Rafe. She certainly knew your grandfather." I sit down in a rickety lawn chair, the rain-rusted joints squealing beneath my bulk.

"Ama?" she asks. "I found her name in my Papaw's things. But he wrote mostly about her husband."

I nod. Hunter steps out on the deck, two steaming mugs of coffee in hand. He glances at the dock but quickly averts his eyes. I want to gather him into my arms and smooth the wrinkles on his brow with my lips. He's looked quite haunted since we boarded the boat.

I take the lead up the ladder, my cellphone in my hand. "We are on our way," the 9-1-1 operator assures me, her voice muffled; I inadvertently had my finger over the speaker output. I adjust my grip, looking to Haley to point me in the right direction.

She tilts her chin toward the bow of the boat, and I continue onward.

When I turn the corner, I nearly step on Renner. Oh god, he's dead, I think, before his body spasms. Myoclonic jerks ripple up and down his limbs, his lips pucker and release.

"The knife," Haley gasps. "He's going to sever his spinal cord, if he hasn't already." The hilt glints, reflecting the warm colors of the sunrise. She's right. I kneel, placing my hands on either side of Renner's head, holding him still. He's cold, his eyes looking past me—through me.

"Hey, Ren," I soothe. "I've got you, buddy. The ambulance is coming." I don't think he can hear me, but I continue to babble, stroking his smooth, bald head until his muscles relax, and he lies still. I try very hard not to look at the blade, nor the thin red line traversing his throat from earlobe to earlobe.

Leigh is sending a message. This was not a wolfish kill but a patently human one.

Hunter suddenly throws himself against the rail, heaving over the side. His knuckles blanch as he vomits into the sea, and when he finally straightens, his face is splotchy and tear-streaked. "Why isn't the ambulance here yet?" he groans.

"They are turning onto Bird's Nest now," the operator says, and sure enough, there's a distant sound of sirens that follows. Within moments, blue-and-red lights strafe across the sand.

Renner starts thrashing again, and I grip his skull tightly, rubbing his jawline with my thumbs. When they pull up dockside, the flashing lights play across his face, making him appear ghoulish.

Despite her resistance, Haley takes the proffered coffee mug. It's one of my favorites: a robin's egg blue with an ornate handle embellished with filigree. She wraps her hands around it, letting the warmth soak into her palms. Hunter hands the second mug—beige, embossed with the Ebb and Flow logo—to me. I take a sip.

"They're here," Hunter says. "I just heard the car pull up. I called Candy, too."

Haley jerks, coffee sloshing into her lap. "Candy is coming here?"

"She's on her way," Hunter replies. "Leigh saw her last night. She's not safe at the loft."

There's a commotion inside the house as the front door opens. Ama shuffles in, her hand resting on Toby's elbow, and Alexandre taking up the rear, leaning heavily on his cane. Haley rises, holding her coffee cup against her chest. "That's Ama, isn't it?"

"That's her," I reply, smiling at my grandmother through the pane of glass. She looks particularly vibrant today, with color in her cheeks and her shoulders squared. Toby leads Ama out onto the back deck, and I rise so the old matriarch can take my seat.

"How's Renner?" Ama asks without preamble. Her eyes rest on the dock. Two policemen stand just abreast of the police tape, paper coffee cups in hand. The sea air offers up bits and pieces of their conversation, tossing it up the beach: "gruesome," "crime of passion," "almost cut his head clean off." The last bit is accompanied by a crude gesture, a thumb dragged from ear to ear, a tongue sticking out for cartoonish effect.

"Alive," I reply. "I said I was his next of kin. They should call me with an update soon." I pat my pocket, feeling the rectangle of cool metal therein. "Haley here saved his life."

"I didn't," Haley insists. "I was just in the right place at the right time." She casts her eyes downward, tapping her nails against her coffee cup.

Ama examines the young woman. "Just like your grandfather," she remarks with a wistful smile. "You're the spitting image of him, you know. He always played down everything, too. He never wanted to take credit. It embarrassed him."

Haley presses her lips together. "I don't want to be compared to him, ma'am."

"Oh?"

"He was a *murderer*." She spits out the last word, as though it is alkaline on her tongue, bitter.

141

CHAPTER TWENTY
(HALEY)

———◁◆▷———

N o one moves, nor speaks. Then, Ama laughs, the
sound akin to a jangling silver bell. "Darling,
that's not giving him much credit, is it?"

I place the mug on the porch rail. I'm gripping
it so tightly I fear it will shatter in my hands. Does
Ama not believe me? "I saw his journal," I insist. "He
killed humans in Sevierville, Ridgerton, and here, in
Wharton, too."

"You're partially right," Ama concedes. "Samuel
was rabid, and he was a menace. But he also stopped,
which I've never seen before or since. He and my husband made a pact, and Sam kept his word."

"He saddled me with this body—this hunger," I say,
embarrassed when my lips tremble. "He made me into
what I am."

"A beautiful wolf-girl, who saved a man last night?"
Ama asks serenely.

"I nearly killed somebody because I was hungry," I
cry, the tears now coming unabated. I feel raw, flayed
open like an autopsy. I hate that everyone is looking at

me, that my backdrop is a snarl of police tape and the pop of flashbulbs. "I didn't ask for this body."

"No one chooses to be born," Ama replies gently. "Perhaps, we should talk in private, little one. Help me up, Angus." She reaches up with one gnarled arm, waiting patiently for the enormous Alpha to haul her up. "Come, child."

I follow her into the house, surprised by the sudden chill indoors. I rub my arms, patting down the goose flesh sprouting there. Angus takes Ama to his bedroom, helping her sit on an overstuffed armchair in the corner. There's nowhere else to sit, save for the unmade bed, so I stand awkwardly. Angus offers me a small reassuring smile before leaving, shutting the French doors behind him.

Ama rests her hands primly in her lap, looking at me with cobalt-colored eyes. Despite their difference in stature, she looks so much like her grandson. They are certainly imbued with the same sort of kinetic energy, as though every cell within them is vibrating; it's a sort of powerful aura that makes it hard to meet their eyes, and even harder to look away. "Are you frightened, child?" she asks.

I am terribly frightened, but I'm not entirely sure how to verbalize it. It's not quite a fear of what has happened, but of what I am capable of in my wolfish flesh. I saw a glimpse of it that night with Tara. It was a cannonball across the bow, a warning shot. *This can get so much worse, can't you see?* I nod.

"I never knew Sam kept a diary," Ama muses. "I'm sure it was strange to see him like that."

"It was all I've ever seen of him," I reply. "He lived with us for the last five years, but we weren't close. I resented him."

"Because he was wolfish, and you were, too." Ama rests her chin on her palm, tapping her fingers against her thin lips.

"And I'm so hungry," I add. "My mother, grandfather—no one else said they felt anything like it. I didn't realize I was like *him* until I read his journal."

"You said you hurt someone. Were they the only one?"

I nod. "I was never wolfish, not *ever*, not if I could help it. Except—"

Gina rolls over in bed, resting her cheek on her forearms. "Run with me tonight," she cajoles. I lean close and kiss her forehead, tasting the sheen of her sweat on my lips. We are both breathless, spent from vigorous lovemaking mere moments ago.

"You know I can't," I murmur. I try to act nonchalant, not wanting to provoke her. I don't want to fight, not tonight. We've had such a nice evening.

"You won't," she amends. "You certainly can." There's an edge to her voice, the disappointment jagged like a saw blade. "C'mon, Hale."

I shake my head.

Gina groans theatrically, sitting up. The covers pool around her tapered waist, revealing her svelte long lines and perky breasts. "This self-hating thing used to be kind of sexy, but now, it's a bore."

"I'll be here when you get home," I say sweetly, slipping a hand under the sheets and up the curve of

her thigh. I want her to stop looking at me like I'm a disappointment. Though, I suppose it's second nature for her now. I'm a lead balloon, dragging her down into the weeds.

Gina snags my wrist in a hand that is suddenly a paw, twisting just enough for a painful zing to shoot up to my elbow. "You're pathetic," she snarls. "How could anyone possibly be scared of you—the only one who's scared is you.*"*

"You're hurting me," I manage, nostrils flaring. The dormant wolf awakens, her teeth cutting through my gums.

Gina doesn't loosen her grip. She transforms into her wolfish body, all sinew and thick, sable fur. Her muzzle nearly touches my nose as she leans close, pulling her lips away from her gums. "Pathetic," she spits.

"Stop it," I manage, keenly aware of the fur sprouting on my abdomen, up the slope of my breasts. "Leave me alone, Gee." I tug my arm out of her grip, but she grabs both of my wrists now, dragging them up above my head. She pins me to the mattress. Her rough tongue slides up my cheek leaving behind wetness and a rash akin to razor burn.

"Give in," she croons. "You are a wolf, aren't you? Act like a fucking wolf, Campbell." My jaw unhinges, my pitiful "no!" dying in my throat. The pain is immense, and tears spring to my eyes. I'm unaccustomed to it, and it feels like I am dying. I hope I die. The wolf can't get out if my heart stops, if my lungs deflate, if my nerve synapses deaden.

But I don't die. The pain rolls over and through me until I soak the mattress with sweat. My vision goes grey, wobbly, Gina's snout coming in and out of focus. Suddenly, I can smell everything: Gina's breath, the latent odor of our arousal, and beyond it, the apartment next door where a family with a small child lives. The baby's room is on the other side of the drywall; we hear her, sometimes, cooing in her crib, calling "mama" when she awakens from a nap.

I can smell her.

"No," I growl, jabbing my knee into Gina's abdomen. I want her off me. I want to lock myself in the bathroom and take deep breaths until the fur finally recedes. Gina releases my wrists, seemingly satisfied by my completed transformation. I roll away from her, panting. "You're cruel," I spit.

"I'm setting you free," she replies. But I feel all the more tethered than before, a prisoner. "We're going to hunt. Get up."

I have no choice. We creep out of Knoxville proper. It's just past midnight, and our apartment complex butts up against the city's most popular haunt: market square. We head South, skulking in the shadows as we cross Henley Street Bridge. We have to crouch against the spindle railings when automobiles pass, my nose pressed against Gina's haunch as we walk single-file.

Finally, we reach our destination: High Ground Park. Gina gives me an impish grin, nipping my shoulder with her teeth. But I pin my ears against my skull, mute. We follow the trail for some time, passing remnants of the Civil War: rifle trenches, a cannon redoubt, and a road—no wider than a game trail. I inadvertently step on a marker for the long-decimated Fort Higley, which is now little more than an expanse of grass and ancient oak trees.

It doesn't take us long to find a small herd of deer in the distance, grazing. There's a knock-kneed fawn with them, and the half-moon paints her dapples silver. A big buck stands at attention, his muscular neck swiveling from left to right. After a moment, he dips his cuneal head toward the earth, snagging a mouthful of grass. The fawn seems unphased by the late hour, bounding around the does with the sort of energy afforded only to the very young.

Gina and I settle into the grass near a stone wall. The long strands tickle my snout, and I huff. "Ready?" Gina asks.

"I'm not going," I snap.

"Suit yourself," she snickers. "But think about it… it's nearly autumn, and they are preparing for winter. They've got an extra layer of fat on them now." I think of hot meat with a silky veneer, so sumptuous, it melts in one's mouth. I imagine the greasiness of it coating my chin, making my fingers slick. God.

When Gina leaps over the wall, I am only a second behind. I don't realize I'm in pursuit until my paws touch the earth on the other side. The herd turns tail as one unit, bounding through the gnarled oaks on nimble hooves. The fawn is ushered to the center of the group; they will keep her safe with their bodies.

Gina yips, her ears swiveling toward a doe who isn't quite keeping up. She runs with her head down, square teeth bared, desperation in every huff and puff. Gina lunges, threading between the herd and the ailing deer. The doe nearly runs straight into me, and I close my jaws on her flank.

Blood pours into my mouth, coating my throat. It's hot, brackish, and thick like mud. For a moment, unparalleled pleasure courses through my core, then the deer trips. I am thrown off balance, and we tumble together, a dervish of hoof, fur, and claw.

When we are finally still, she tries to regain her feet. But her leg is broken, her cracked femur visible through a tangle of torn flesh. The doe raises her thick neck, searching for her herd. She bleats. I loom over her, her blood crusting on my snout. I don't hesitate again, sinking my teeth into her neck, finding the thick cord of her jugular amidst the fibrous muscle.

When her last breath squeaks from her deflating lungs, my body convulses in ecstasy. Then, I tear her apart.

Ama sits quietly, listening to me prattle on. My thoughts curl into and around each other. I tug on bits and pieces of memory, untying knots, laying them flat for Ama to see. I tell her about attacking Tara, the ever-present nightmares, even meeting Candace Bailey.

"It sounds like," Ama finally says, when I exhaust myself, "you have been battling with yourself for a very long time."

"Yes," I breathe.

"It *also* sounds like you have been torturing yourself," she muses, "punishing yourself even when there was nothing to penalize."

I think of the nights spent curled up in my childhood bedroom, my wolfish body trembling on the sagging mattress. She—*I*—just wanted to run, and instead, I tightened the collar, double-knotted the leash. "I never asked anyone if it was normal, the *hunger*," I murmur, picking at my cuticles.

Ama rises. She shuffles toward me, taking my hands in hers. "I think," she says, looking up into my eyes, "we are all very much afraid. Our instincts are so deeply ingrained in us, that sometimes, they collide with our more human traits. You are doing just fine, child."

CHAPTER TWENTY-ONE
(CANDY)

———— ◁◆▷ ————

Briiing, briiing, my cellphone trills.

I roll over in bed, blindly reaching for it on my cluttered nightstand. I touch a bottle of Excedrin Migraine and an empty glass ashtray before my fingers rest on the vibrating phone. "Hello?" I mumble, jabbing the screen. I crack open my eyelids, groaning when bright light streams full pelt into my retinas. I left the blinds open the night before, and the sun leans into the easterly-facing windows. I pull the bedsheets up over my head.

"Candy." It's Hunter. "You need to come over." He sounds tired, strained. I think he's outside; the wind pummels the receiver, making it sound as though he's cloistered inside a wind tunnel.

I peel the sheets back, casting a glance at Haley's temporary living quarters. She isn't asleep on the couch. The blankets and pillows are folded on the armrest, just as they were the night before. *Last night*. I think of her mouth on mine, her fingers inside me, and my stomach flip-flops. "What's going on?" I ask, suppressing a yawn.

"Just come," he replies. I can hear Angus' deep rumble, but I can't make out the words. "Now," he clarifies. The call disconnects.

I hurriedly dress, scraping my hair up into a frizzy knot. As I tie my sneakers, I find my hands are shaking. Hunter's clipped tone was very atypical, and after the frightening events of the night before, I'm not sure what I am walking into. It certainly didn't sound like an impromptu breakfast between siblings.

Downstairs, the cafe operates as normal, Renee and Maria behind the counter. "Can I get a cup to go?" I ask Maria, gesturing at the pot of steeping black coffee.

Maria pours the steaming liquid into a cardboard cup, securing the lid. "We got a weird phone call from Hunter," she says. "He was supposed to open with us. Is he okay?" Hunter never misses a shift. I feel queasy.

"I'm not sure," I reply truthfully. "I'm heading over there right now."

I trot out into the street, easing behind the wheel of my car. It's muggy, though its only in the mid-70s, and the metal seatbelt latch burns my fingers. I curse under my breath, blowing on my fingertips. The car starts with a cough, and I pull sharply into traffic, ignoring the agitated bleating of a horn behind me. My body feels loose, like a ragdoll tossed into the air. I'm not entirely sure where I will land.

Hurry, Hunter had said. Did something happen to dad? He was slow-going last time I saw him, leaning heavily on me as thought I was a crutch. I had blamed it on the uneven terrain, but perhaps, it was something more. His hair was more salt than pepper. His crow's feet were veritable trenches. Before mom's flowers floated past the buoys, I noticed his tears diverted through his wrinkles, like a river flowing through a canyon.

A tiny whimper escapes me, gripping the steering wheel until my knuckles blanch white. When I reach the turn onto Bird's Nest, I gun the engine, bouncing on the gravel road. The coffee jostles and spills, soaking the passenger seat.

Hunter's bungalow looks just as it always does. The exterior is a cheerful yellow, two Adirondack chairs crowding the front porch. I park alongside the mailbox, my tire scraping against the post and knocking it slightly off-kilter. I don't bother to straighten it, out of desperation to find my brother.

Angus opens the front door, stepping out onto the patio. He is wearing sweatpants and a sleeveless tee, his arms thick with knotted muscle. His forehead and left eye are swollen, knotted stitches adorning his brow. "Candace," he murmurs. "Thank you for coming."

"What's going on?" My mouth feels dry, my tongue thick and adhering to the roof of my mouth.

"Come in," he says, stepping aside. He's being evasive, avoiding my question. Angus propels me into the house, his hand on the small of my back.

It's dark and cool inside. Goosebumps prickle on my arms, and I rub them. "Tell me what's going on," I exclaim.

Angus locks the door behind me, sliding the deadbolt. "Come sit down," he urges, leading me into the living room.

There's nowhere to sit. The couch is occupied by a young woman with short-cropped hair, her hands resting on her round belly; an old man with a cane between his knees; and Hunter, who pops up when he sees me. Ama Chilton sits in Angus' favorite leather recliner, her eyes half-lidded as though unable to stay awake.

Hunter is speaking to me, but I'm not listening. I'm looking past him, at the woman sitting on the ottoman, her back a parenthesis. *Haley.* She avoids my eyes, her arms wrapped tightly around her midsection.

"Last night," Hunter says, getting my attention with a snap of his fingers, "the wolf that attacked us attacked one of Angus' pack mates and left him for dead. We are all in danger."

"We?" I ask dumbly. I don't know what I have to do with any of this. I'm...*normal.* I only just stumbled into this world, and I am more than happy to step back out of it. *And why is Haley here?*

"Leigh saw you last night," Hunter continues, "and she knows you're my sister."

Haley finally meets my unrelenting gaze, her lips pressed together. She looks exhausted, dark bags beneath her eyes. Her hair sticks to her sweaty forehead. Hunter follows my gaze. "Your friend saved Renner's life. He would have died if she hadn't found him."

I know Renner. He's a regular customer at the cafe. Without fail, he orders a hot London Fog with an extra splash of steamed milk. "More milk than tea, dear, that's right," he would say, nodding approvingly as I poured. He told jokes to Renee and the other younger baristas, laughing before he could share the punchline.

"Why is pirating so addictive?" he'd ask. "*Because*," he'd chortle, putting a few dollars into the tip jar, "they say once you lose your first hand, you get *hooked*!"

"That woman attacked Renner?" I ask, still uncomprehending.

"Leigh," Hunter corrects. "She stabbed him in the neck and tried to strangle him. He's in the hospital now—in surgery."

"I was out," Haley says, "just walking, after..." She grimaces, chewing at her lip. I think of Haley's hands on my breasts, and my cheeks grow hot. I hope no one can see. "...after we *talked*. I heard the man calling for help. My phone died, so I ran to the nearest house— this one."

"It was kismet," Ama Chilton suddenly says, her voice honeyed. I had thought she was dozing; she had barely moved in the minutes I've been in the room. "Though, wolves always find each other, don't they?"

Angus sighs. "Granny," he sighs. "Candy doesn't know."

"I don't know *what*?" Everyone is looking at me. The teenage girl's eyes are saucers. She mouths *holy shit* under her breath.

Ama shrugs her thin shoulders. "She's in this now; surely you weren't going to leave her in the dark?" She's talking to Haley, who looks as though she's been slapped.

After a moment, Haley rises from the ottoman, reaching for my arm. "Can we talk?"

CHAPTER TWENTY-TWO
(HALEY)

———◁◆▷———

Through the closed French doors, I can hear the hum of the wolf pack's conversation. I stare at the doors, hands in my lap, sitting on the very edge of Hunter and Angus' bed. Candy sits beside me, our shoulders touching. "What is *going on*?" she asks. "Last night, you just *left*. Now you're at my brother's house. Please talk to me."

I want to tell her, but I'm frightened.

Tentative, she touches my hand, giving my fingers a squeeze. "I," she continues, "I really like you, Haley."

"You know about Angus, right?" I ask. "What he can do—what he is?"

"I saw it," she murmurs. "He fought that other one—the one who hurt Renner. That's why I was so freaked out last night. It's why I kissed you."

"I knew about Angus when I met him. We could smell each other." Candy stiffens beside me, making both of our shoulders rise around our ears. "We're the same," I add, the words toppling over one another in a single rush.

Candy rises from the bed, looking down at me. "This is all so *strange*," she exclaims. "It's like I woke up and everyone decided to play a prank on me." Her lips tremble, betraying the emotional tsunami within her.

"I'm sorry," I say, "and I'm sorry for leaving last night. I was scared, because—"

Candy waits for me to continue, looking down at me.

"—I really like you," I finish. *And I don't want to hurt you.*

Candy sits back down, surveying me with dark eyes. She picks at the hem of her cutoffs, tugging on the loose strings. "I like you too," she whispers. "Despite what you are, I like you."

Hesitantly, I touch her face, brushing her bangs off her forehead. Her eyelids droop, her lips parting just slightly as she exhales. Then, I kiss her, pressing my lips chastely against hers. When I pull away, her cheeks are rose-colored.

There's a knock on the door, and it eases open just enough for Hunter to peek in. "The hospital just called." Distantly, I can hear someone weeping.

Candy grips my hand, and we wordlessly file out of the room.

The young girl—Toby—is crying, wiping at her big wet eyes with the neckline of her t-shirt. Angus paces the room, his hands deep in his pockets, his eyes downcast. Everyone gives him a wide berth. "Renner didn't survive surgery," Hunter murmurs. The young man I met in the coffee shop looks as though he's aged ten years in ten minutes. His whole body droops, and he sniffles.

"We're going to look for Leigh," Angus announces abruptly. "Alexandre, Haley, and I. She's injured, so she'll probably lay low in the woods."

"Me?" I sputter. "I'm not—" But my words die mid-breath. *I'm not in this pack.* Like it or not, I'm entrenched in this. Finding Renner cemented my place here. Still, I don't want to go on this hunt. It would mean I would have to wear my pelt and become *her*.

Alexandre sets aside his cane and stands. It takes him a moment to straighten his spine, but when he's up, his viridescent eyes are clear and stalwart. "I'm ready," he says. "Allons-y."

Hunter shakes his head. "She could be anywhere. There are miles of forests. Leigh could be at a *hotel* for all we know."

Angus remove his shirt, revealing thick musculature and skin made golden by the sun. "I can't wait around—not this time. I made that mistake before."

"Angus—" Hunter presses his lips together.

But, Angus' face contorts, his jaw sawing from side-to-side as it elongates into a snout. He rolls his shoulders forward, and pearlescent fur erupts upon them, trickling down his back.

"Jesus," Candy breathes beside me.

The old man follows suit, his bones snapping like matchsticks. He nearly falls over, but Toby grabs his elbow, supporting him.

Candy turns away, looking sick. It's not a beautiful thing—the transformation. It's violent, stomach-churning. Surely, she can imagine the sensations involved. Has she ever broken a bone, stubbed a toe, torn a muscle, lost a tooth, or dragged her nails down a chalkboard?

Hunter, who I imagine has seen this before, casts his eyes toward the ceiling.

It's my turn. Angus looks at me expectantly, sitting back on his haunches. His eyes are striking against his white fur, like two enormous sapphires. Hunter pats the enormous wolf's muscular shoulder, tangling his fingers in the thick fur. Does Hunter realize how much danger he is in? Surely, Angus has thought of his rabbit heart, a staccato under his palm. Surely, Angus has pressed his lips against Hunter's skin, and thought, "just one, little taste." Does he fantasize about it, the twin flames of pleasure and sustenance driving him to orgasm?

I step into my fur in fits and starts—threading the wolf's leash through my fingers. My kneecaps pop backward first, and I fall to the carpet. Dimly, I am aware of Candy's hands squeezing my shoulders, but the pain yanks me away from my body. It feels as though I'm strung above a fire, turning on a spit. I'm burning, my joints sparking, my blood turning to skin-blistering oil. *Don't touch me, or you'll be burned,* I want to tell her.

Finally, the kaleidoscope before my eyes comes into focus, and she is all I see. Candy kneels beside me, concern etched into the corners of her eyes, the ridge of her brow. "Haley?" she asks.

"I'm okay," I manage through wolfish gums and teeth.

"You're….beautiful," Candy breathes, her fingers brushing against my snout. I can smell her, that floral perfume I've come to adore. She strokes my cheeks, smoothing the pewter fur. "I'm not scared," she murmurs, though the lilt in her voice betrays her somewhat.

She's trying to be brave. I want to try, too.

I nudge her cheek with my nose.

"Let's run," Angus barks, impatient.

It's not quite noon, and three enormous bipedal wolf-creatures will certainly be conspicuous. But Angus appears to have a plan. We leave out of the front door one-by-one, crossing the two-lane gravel road and into the deep ditch on the other side. The ground in the ditch is soft and damp, and we squelch through the mud, shielded by the long grass and cattails. We follow Bird's Nest down to its abrupt terminus: a copse of trees. Once therein, we break into an easy lope, heading deeper into the foliage.

"There are miles of woodlands on the north and west sides of Wharton. Leigh used to hunt out here when she was in the pack," Angus says.

"You said she was hurt?" I ask.

"I think I took a good bite or two when she cornered Hunter and Candy," he says, speaking easily despite our quick pace.

Conversely, Alexandre is silent, panting, his long, pink tongue lolling. He's missing quite a few teeth, and those remaining are yellow and dull. "The...blind," Alexandre puffs.

Angus slows, and so do I. Ahead, there's a metal ladder, lashed to the trunk of a sourwood tree. It's a strange, very *human,* relic, certainly not something I expect to see deep within the forest. All the more odd, is that the ladder seemingly leads nowhere. It simply terminates at the top rung. "It's for deer hunting," Angus explains. "Thankfully, the blinds aren't occupied for another month. But a hunter will sit up there, point his rifle at the clover *there,* and wait."

The area is thick with clover, smelling faintly of vanilla. I shiver, examining the ladder. It seems so cold, shooting the animals from above. I try to imagine nibbling on the sweet clover, then, pow: nothingness. Though, I amend, it does sound much less painful than being torn apart by claw and tooth.

I feel queasy.

"Leigh used to hunt near the water tower. We're a mile out," Angus says. He takes off again, but somewhat slower this time. He keeps one ear swiveled toward the elder wolf, mindful of his frailty.

The water tower becomes visible within a half-mile, a rust-colored smudge on the horizon coming sharply into focus. The town name is written in cursive, the letters faded. I can barely see the loop of the 'r' even as we are standing just beneath the concrete supports.

"This place has a lot of history," Angus tells me. "My granny always tells the story of meeting my grandfather here, seeing him in his fur for the first time." He turns his wedge-shaped head toward me. "It's also where he said goodbye to your grandfather, before he went back to Tennessee and started a family."

"I can't imagine a nice lady like Ama Chilton being close with my grandfather," I admit.

"Ama is a good judge of character." Angus grins, bearing his teeth.

"What did she think of Leigh?" Alexandre asks, scratching at his ear with his back leg. Dandruff floats around his head like an aura.

"She had liked her," Angus admits. He circles the supports, pressing his nose to the ground. "Though, a lot has changed in the last few months, and Leigh lost someone close to her."

"And she blames you for it?" I ask, curious. I'm still not entirely sure what Leigh's motives are. To me, she's a faceless entity, motivated by anger. I can't see how someone could stab anyone if they aren't extraordinarily enraged. It's an intimate crime—exceedingly personal. She wanted to leave a message. Even I, a complete stranger, could parse it: "fuck you."

"I killed him," Angus murmurs. "Leigh hasn't been here," he adds, completing his circuit of the supports.

"Candy said someone shot you."

"Yes. But it was a perfect storm of events. Or maybe, it was orchestrated. I don't think I'll ever be entirely sure. The important part is that James was rabid. He wanted to kill Hunter when he discovered we were together, and I killed him for it."

I can't help but think of Samuel. "Was there no fixing him? Ama said my grandfather was cured."

Angus shrugs. "I didn't know such a thing was possible. I wish I had known. I really do."

CHAPTER TWENTY-THREE
(CANDY)

H unter stands with the curtain bunched in his hand, watching the street. The three wolves left ten minutes ago, and Bird's Nest remained tranquil. No one bolted down the street in hysterics, nor charged outside armed with a beach umbrella fashioned into a lance. They weren't spotted.

Wordlessly, Toby shuffles into Hunter's kitchen, looking through the cabinets. She returns with a box of Cheez-Its, popping one of the squares into her mouth. She offers them to Ama, Hunter, and me in turn, but we all shake our heads. "Suit yourselves," she mutters, sitting back down onto the plush couch. "We could be here for a while." She balances the box on her baby bump.

"Leigh could be anywhere," Hunter groans, exasperated. "I feel like Angus is—" He presses his lips together so hard they blanch as he sinks down on the ottoman. His knees bump against his chest, making him look like a child.

"He's chasing his tail," Ama says sagely. "But who can blame him?" She glances pointedly at the large sliding glass door, through which we can see the flat, aluminum roof of the houseboat.

It's strange, being so close to a violent crime scene; I feel like a voyeur. Though, I've felt like I've been intruding all day.

Suddenly, Hunter's phone rings. He answers it, turning his back to the room, and by extension, us. "Yeah?" His rounded shoulders straighten into a flat plane, and he curses. "I'll be right there."

After he hangs up, he pinches the bridge of his nose. "There's a fire at the cafe."

"Jesus," I breathe. "Is everyone okay?"

"I don't know." He grabs his keys from a hook near the front door. "I have to go."

Toby lurches to her feet, the box of Cheez-Its tumbling to the floor. "Angus wanted us to stay put," she says in a rush.

"My livelihood is burning," Hunter replies shortly. "I can't sit here."

"I'm going too," I say. I can't help but think of dark, oily smoke filling up my loft, covering all of my belongings with gray ash.

Ama takes Toby's hand, giving the younger woman a little tug. "We'll stay here," she soothes. "We can send Angus and Haley to the cafe when they return."

Hunter doesn't seem to be listening. He's already out the door and onto the porch steps. A current of hot air pours into the foyer, clouding my glasses. I follow him to his Camry, throwing open the passenger side door and sliding in. The leather sticks to my sweaty thighs.

He shifts into reverse, backing out of the driveway. He nearly hits my SUV, and I wince. "What caused the fire?" I ask. We're speeding, the tires grinding against the gravel with a violent *crunch*. The bungalows of Bird's Nest quickly give way to the sights of Wharton proper.

"Not sure," Hunter replies. "Renee just said the fire department was there." He coughs into his fist, as though it can hide the trembling of his lips, the muscle twitching spasmodically just beneath his eye. He's anxious.

We see the smoke when we turn onto Main Street from Leland Drive. "Oh, Hunt," I breathe when I spot the thick column rising about the buildings.

Hunter says nothing. Instead, he honks the horn at a couple taking too long to cross the street.

We can't drive further than Seaside Books. There's a police cordon, and beyond it, two massive fire trucks. Hunter lurches from the car without turning off the engine, ducking beneath the tape. I reach over, loosing the keys from the ignition. For a moment, I can't quite get myself to leave the car. My legs feel leaden. I don't want to see what's become of the cafe. As much as I resented it for my entire life, it's my home. My parents and Hunter poured their lifeblood into it. Even I did, albeit less so.

Finally, I get out and duck underneath the tape, ignoring a police officer who asks me to stop, to wait. "My house is on fire," I shout over my shoulder. I am surprised by the giggle that follows suit. *What a bizarre day!*

From the sidewalk, Ebb and Flow looks largely unharmed. The facade is unaffected. Even the a-frame chalkboard is in its place on the sidewalk, advertising the current special: a free biscotti with the purchase of a medium coffee. Renee had attempted to draw a biscotti, but it looked more like a carrot. A hose snakes over the sidewalk, lying flat; the water isn't on.

The front door opens, and Hunter is corralled out by a fireman. The fireman holds his arms out wide, as if Hunter is a wild mustang he is attempting to tame. "It's not safe!" the fireman hisses through his respirator. "We need to finish our inspection."

Hunter sighs. "Fine, but I'll be *right here*. I want an update as soon as you have one."

"It'll be a while, Mr. Bailey," the fireman replies without apology. He gives my brother a final nod before heading back inside.

Hunter's face is wet with sweat, and he wipes it away with his palm. "It originated in the kitchen," he tells me. "Or at least, that's where most of the damage is. I only got a glimpse."

"Hunter!" Renee trots up from the opposite side of the street. Her face is contorted with emotion, her chin dimpled. "I don't know what happened," she blubbers. "One minute I was making drinks, the next Emanuel ran into the dining area shouting for everyone to get out."

I look for Emmanuel in the crowd. "Where is Emmanuel?" I easily find Maria and the dishwasher, Tristan, but the tall, tattooed chef is nowhere to be seen.

"He's over at the ambulance. They wanted to have a look at him. His clothes were singed." Renee gestures at an idling ambulance; its back doors open. Someone sits on the bumper, an EMT standing over them.

Hunter and I head over to the ambulance.

Emmanuel looks up as we approach, his lined face smeared with ash. "Hey, boss. Hey, Candy," he grunts. The EMT holds Emmanuel's wrist gently in her gloved hand, pouring water from a plastic Aquafina bottle over his palm.

"Are you okay?" I ask.

Emmanuel shrugs. "Just a superficial burn. No big deal."

"It's a second-degree burn," the EMT gently corrects him. "I'm going to wrap this now, but you really need to follow up with your doctor. I wish you would let me take you to the ER."

Emmanuel raises his eyebrows at me, crinkling the blown-out teardrop tattoo beneath his waterline. "I've had worse."

"What happened in there?" Hunter asks. He sits on the tailgate beside his employee, resting his hand on the older man's drooping shoulder.

The EMT dries Emmanuel's hand, then slathers Bacitracin on the half-dollar sized patch of burned skin. Emmanuel, despite his bravado, grimaces. "I am not sure, to tell you the truth. I was pulling a batch of macarons from the oven, and when I turned around, the trashcan was on fire. It was like someone slipped in and threw a match. I had the back door open, like usual, because the kitchen air was hot."

"Did you hear or see anyone?" Hunter asks.

"No," Emmanuel replies. "But I had my earbuds in." He taps the small Bose earbud in his right ear. "I was listening to Dateline," he adds, an afterthought.

As the EMT loosely wraps Emmanuel's hand in gauze, Emmanuel gives Hunter a sidelong look. "I'm sorry, boss. I tried to put it out, but it spread too quickly. So then, I just got everyone out of there."

"You have nothing to apologize for, man," Hunter murmurs. "You're a hero—truly."

A firefighter approaches the ambulance, his helmet tucked under his arm. He reeks of smoke, and his face is oily. "Mr. Bailey?" he asks, his thick mustache quivering when he speaks.

"That's me," Hunter replies, standing.

"I'm Chief Jeong. Looks like the fire was set. We found evidence of an accelerant in the trash can. Do you have any reason to believe someone would be targeting you or your business?"

Hunter pales. He glances at me, and in that instant, I understand. Leigh still has a bright red target adorning our backs. Scaring us in the alley and attacking Renner wasn't enough. I glance around at the crowd gathered just outside of the cordon. They stand on tiptoes, straining their necks, attempting to get a good view of the goings-ons. I wonder, then, if Leigh is standing there, watching.

We don't get to see the damage until several hours later. Chief Jeong leads Hunter and I inside the cafe. It's hot and stagnant inside; the fire department turned off the electricity. The dining area is relatively unscathed. The kitchen, however, is a husk. The fire burned hot and fast, and the walls are black with soot.

"Oh my god," I breathe.

Hunter is silent, his jaw stiff.

He listens as the chief describes the flames' trajectory, how the accelerant splashed off the trashcan's rim, soaking the wall behind it. The wall had a cork board on it, where Hunter pinned our schedules, the menu, even photos. I can just see the sliver of my cheek in a flame-shredded photograph, still somehow adhered there. I recognize my own freckle, shaped vaguely like an upside-down heart. It was once a photo of me, Renee, and Maria, our faces pressed together so we could fit into the frame.

"What about the loft?" I ask.

"It's intact," Chief Jeong replies. "A lot of smoke damage."

"Can I get a few things?" I ask. "I live there."

"I can take you up," the mustachioed firemen says.

Hunter remains in the kitchen while Chief Jeong and I climb the stairs. True to his word, there is no evidence of fire here, though the walls are blackened. I swipe my finger against the wall, the residue sticking to my skin. It smells strongly of smoke, and my eyes water. I grab a bag, stuffing Haley and I's clothes inside. It feels awkward packing under the watchful eye of a stranger, and I find myself hurrying, not wanting to waste his time.

Within minutes, I shoulder my now-heavy bag. "I'm ready."

Outside, it's a relief to breathe in fresh air. "You and Haley can stay with us," Hunter says, running his hands through his hair. "Of course."

With nothing left to do at the cafe and the sun setting, Hunter and I climb back into his Camry. I can still smell smoke on us, a persistent ghost. "Do you think they found Leigh?" I ask. I can't bear to sit in silence. It feels heavy, like we are being buried alive.

Hunter just sighs.

Suddenly, the back doors of the Camry open, and two people slide inside. It's Angus and Haley.

Angus, sitting behind the driver's seat, leans forward, resting his hands on Hunter's shoulders. "I'm so sorry," he murmurs. He's only wearing a pair of board shorts, much too small for him; the fabric constricts his thick thighs, making them look like overstuffed sausages. I think they are my brother's. He was clearly in a hurry to get here. "Hunter, I'm so sorry. Ama told us what happened."

"Did you find her?" Hunter asks, not bothering to acknowledge his boyfriend. His hands remain on the steering wheel, his eyes focused on the street. In the hours since we arrived, the street had cleared significantly. The cordon has been taken down, the emergency vehicles have vanished, and the sidewalk is open for pedestrians. Ebb and Flow, however, is dark, police tape and structural integrity warnings decorating the locked front door.

Angus sighs. "No."

"Well, she was *here*," Hunter snarls.

CHAPTER TWENTY-FOUR
(ANGUS)

—◁◆▷—

The ride back to the bungalow is chilly. In the driveway, Hunter gets out and heads inside without waiting for the rest of us, slamming the door. I wince, the sound and its echo are a one-two punch to the abdomen. "Let me get you two settled in the guest room," I say to Haley and Candy.

I insist on carrying their bag inside. Hunter is not in the living room nor the kitchen, and our bedroom door is closed. I lead the women into the small guest room, placing their bag on the bedspread. It's a small room, though it has an en-suite bathroom. Hunter and I have largely used it for storage. I push several boxes out of the way, folding up my woefully underused treadmill.

"Thank you," Candy says. "This is nice." She's being kind—pointedly so. It's as though she can see the slap mark left by Hunter's words and wants to put a salve on it.

"There are fresh towels in the bathroom," I say, offering her a tight smile.

Haley mouths *thanks*, sitting on the edge of the
bed. Since being wolfish, she has been quiet, withdrawn. Her fingers trace the stitching on the comforter,
outlining flowers and bird wings.

I leave the two women alone and cross the living
room to my closed bedroom door. I hesitate. I cannot
fathom what Hunter is feeling right now. His business
is in jeopardy, and his safety is in question. And ostensibly, it's my fault. If I had done what I had to regarding
James, surely none of this would have happened.

Inside, the room is filled with a velvety darkness.
The blinds are drawn, and I can just barely make out
the shape of Hunter beneath the bed linen. He's lying
on his side, facing the wall. I crawl into bed, slipping
under the covers. He doesn't acknowledge me, even
when I cuddle up close, his body heat flush against my
chest. His breathing is deep and even.

"I'm going to fix this," I murmur into his ear, wrapping my arms around his thin frame. He smells like
smoke and sweat.

Hunter just sighs, exhaling so hard his whole
body seems to deflate. I rest my chin on his shoulder,
pressing my lips against his stubbly neck. "I think this
feels worse because I was kind to her," he finally says.

I think of my last conscious moment in the cafe
that fateful morning. Everything felt like it was filtered
through a thick layer of cotton. It was as though I was
the personification of a bruise: blood pooling, ugly to
look at, tender to touch.

I remember Hunter's voice, the way he had said,
"go." He waited, finger poised over the CALL button,
while Leigh and Luka escaped, James' body thrown

over Luka's muscular shoulder. Before I fell into the void, coming to hours later in the hospital, I swear James sneered at me.

"You're a good man," I murmur.

"I thought we were finally in a good place," Hunter continues. "It was all behind us." When he starts to cry, I hold him tight. And when crying exhausts him, his breath quavering, I undress him.

CHAPTER TWENTY-FIVE
(CANDY)

———◁◆▷———

"What was it like?" I ask when we are alone. Dimly, I can hear Angus' footfalls fading away, a door open and close.

"What do you mean?" Haley tucks a strand of hair behind her ear. She looks as tired as I feel, the flesh under her eyes swollen and grey. She chews at her lower lip.

"Being a wolf," I say. "You don't seem to like doing it."

Haley lays back on the mattress, her feet hanging off the bed. "True. I don't like it," she admits, draping her forearm over her eyes. "It's frightening. I feel like I get *lost*."

I lay on my side beside her. Her arm covers her face, but I can see the curve of her cheek, the down-turned corner of her mouth. "It's not that we are two separate people—beings, I mean," Haley continues. "I'm her, and she's me. But sometimes, she can be very loud. The wolf has *needs*. She's hungry all of the time."

The way she says 'hungry' gives me pause. There's a weight implicit therein, like being hungry is cumbersome. When she says the word, her voice wavers just slightly, like she's swallowing a sob. "Haley," I murmur. "You can talk to me."

Haley turns her head and looks into my eyes. Her hand falls to her side. "I don't think so," she whispers.

I feel a little indignant at that. I prop myself up on my elbow, looking down at her. "I think you're underestimating what I'm capable of. I know I'm just a normal, *boring* human, but—"

"You aren't boring," Haley interrupts. "I just don't want you to look at me like I'm a horrible person." She threads her fingers through mine, giving them a gentle squeeze.

"I won't," I promise. "Please talk to me."

Haley sighs. "I told you that I came to Wharton to find someone who knew my grandfather. That was because I found his diary, and what I read scared me. He was wolfish, like me. Like most everyone in my family. But he was the only one who had mentioned the…the…"

"The hunger."

"That's right. And what scared me most was how he acted on that impulse. Candy, he *killed* people." Haley abruptly sits up, and I stare at her sloping back, her hair made frizzy by the mattress. Her hands cover her face, like a toddler hiding from their mother, and she says in a muffled voice, "It was scary because, when I'm wolfish, and sometimes, even when I'm not, I want to do the exact same thing. I have dreams— nightmares—about it."

My body thrums, suddenly aware of my own blood flowing through my veins. My heart is hammering, but I don't move.

"And," she gulps, "after I read his diary, I attacked someone. I think she's okay. I think she survived, but I came here to be cured like my grandfather was."

"He stopped hurting people?" I ask, my mouth dry. My tongue feels far too big for my mouth. But my voice is even, and for that, I'm grateful. I don't want Haley to know I'm scared, that every nerve-ending is screaming *run*.

"Yes," Haley replies. "After meeting Angus' grandfather—Ama, too."

"Can she help you, too?" I ask.

"I don't know," Haley whispers. "I really don't. I hope so."

"Do you think about it when you're with me?" I ask before I lose my never. I think of her hands beneath my shirt, her hot mouth on mine. Her actions said *hungry*, but not quite in the same way.

Haley finally turns to look at me. "Every second. But, Candy, I don't want to hurt you. I just want—I just *wanted*—to make you feel good. I like you."

"Are you thinking about it right now?" I sit up, and we are so close together our breath commingles.

Haley's breath hitches. "Yes," she admits. The admission hangs above us like the blade of a guillotine.

I don't want to run away. I want to tell her about my own secret thoughts; how her hands, her mouth, her tongue brought them into sharp focus. Tentative, I touch her cheek, the pad of my thumb stroking her lower lip. Her lips pull away from her teeth, and for a second, I swear they are sharp like a wolf's. "Are you going to hurt me?" I ask, breathless.

"I don't want to," she replies, which isn't a *no*. She's breathing fast now, as though being chased. Perhaps she is; I feel like the rabbit bounding after the wolf, eager to stick its neck between the predator's jaws.

"Did you hurt that man at The Cove?" I ask. Haley's tongue darts out of her mouth, tapping my thumb. Her whole body shivers.

"No," she replies. "That wasn't me. I swear."

"I believe you."

"Candy," she breathes. "I'm scared."

"Me too," I reply. I lean close, ensnaring her lips with mine. She hesitates but kisses me back, her tongue slithering into my mouth. Haley is wearing shorts, and an oversized Ebb and Flow tee I recognize as my brother's. Her blouse shredded when she transformed; the tatters still on the living room floor, long forgotten. I slide my hand along her long, tapered thigh, just like she did to me the other night. It's my first time touching her—really touching her—and I use her movements as a roadmap.

Haley dips her head and kisses my neck. Her breath is hot on my skin, and I wonder what she's thinking. What do I smell like to her? I imagine her teeth growing sharp, clamping down on my flesh. But all I feel are soft kisses, gentle but insistent.

I press Haley back onto the mattress, unbuttoning her shorts. Her eyes half-lidded, she raises her hips for me, so I can slide the garment down her legs. I can't seem to stop the trembling of my hands as I touch her, and I hope she doesn't notice. Hesitantly, I kiss her upper thighs, each in turn, then I touch the gusset of her underwear with my palm. The fabric is moist.

"Candy—"

I don't know if it's a plea or a warning, but I stroke her lightly through the fabric, watching her face contort. I squeeze my own thighs together, a zing of pleasure coursing through my core.

Haley grasps my hand, stilling my ministrations. "I'm afraid," she gasps. "When you touch me, I feel like I'm going to lose control."

"Do you want me to stop?" She's gripping my hand tightly, but after a moment, her hold loosens. I slip my fingers through hers and move to lay alongside her prone body. "We can stop," I murmur.

"I don't want to," she says, turning onto her side. Her hand rests on my cheek, her thumb tracing the curve of my bottom lip. Hesitantly, I slip my hand beneath her shirt, cupping her small breast. Her lip quirks into a half-smile, and she unbuttons my shorts, pushing them down my thighs until I can kick them off and away.

Haley scoots closer until our bodies touch, her thigh sliding between my legs and coaxing them apart. I pinch her nipple, and she hisses. For the briefest moment, I swear her eyes glow, but she blinks, and the effect is gone. It must have been a trick of the light, a reflection of the half-full moon through the window.

I shuck her shirt up over her head, dipping my head to kiss her breast through her thin cotton bra. She whimpers, her fingers twining in my hair as I push the fabric aside, sucking her pink nipple into my mouth. She arches her back, a soft gasp escaping her lips.

I swirl my tongue around the puckered flesh, then press her onto her back again. I kiss down her flat belly, stopping when my lips brush against the hem of her fuchsia-colored panties.

Haley's hands are still firmly in my hair, and she gives me a nudge. *Please*. Her hips buck.

I can smell her through the fabric, earthy and musky. Gentle, I press my lips against the fabric, kissing the top of her mound. "Cay," Haley breathes.

I slide my tongue along the damp gusset, and her grip on my hair tightens. She nudges me again, urging me without words. I hook my index fingers through the fabric, pulling her underwear down to her knees. She spreads her legs for me and arches her hips.

"Cay," she says again, her voice suddenly texturized like crushed glass. It's her wolfish voice.

Startled, I look up to meet her wide-eyed stare. Her eyes are unquestionably glowing now, two embers in the half-dark room. It reminds me of the eyes of a lion, stalking a goat herder on the Serengeti; I saw the photo in an old, dusty *National Geographic*. The photo frightened me as a child because the predator's intentions were clear. If the man turned his back, he would be dinner. Would Haley do the same to me?

Still, I look away, kissing each thigh in turn. She doesn't pounce. Even her grip on my hair loosens, her fingertips gently massaging my scalp. "We can stop," I remind her, my breath hot on her sex.

"Please don't," she groans, and when I lick her there, her orgasm is immediate. Her legs clasp tight around my ears, and she bucks her hips until her body loosens. When I come up for air, breathless, I am surprised to see her once-naked flesh is obscured by silvery fur. When her lips part, I can see the edge of keen, skin-rending and bone-crushing canines.

For a moment, fear paralyzes me. My breath catches in my throat, and I am certain I won't be able to take in more air ever again. I will suffocate here. But then, the moment passes, and I crawl up to lay beside her. She turns her face away, embarrassed by her body's response to our lovemaking. "You're okay," I assure her. "We're okay." I stroke her shoulder, surprised both by how silky smooth her fur is and how steady my hand is.

I wake up early, the squawking of seagulls outside jerking me out of my slumber. The sun pushes its fingers through the slats, and I can see the silhouettes of my avian alarm clocks as they squabble. I roll away with a sleepy moan, reaching blindly for Haley. I expect to touch her naked skin, made cool by the oscillating ceiling fan. But instead, my hands touch fur.

I freeze. The wolf—*Haley*, I remind myself—is asleep, her chin resting on her front paws. She is enormous, and the mattress sags beneath her weight. Haley's words the night before pour over me like cold water. *Every second*, she'd said. Is she dreaming of tearing me apart? If she wakes, will the wolf act before the human locked inside gets her bearings?

I slowly ease out of bed, wincing when the mattress springs twang beneath me. While her trigonal ears twitch in my direction, she doesn't wake. I grab for clothes on the floor, not taking my eyes off her. I step into my panties, shorts, my phone heavy in the pocket) and throw the shirt I wore the day before over my head. It still reeks of smoke. Haley doesn't stir when I open the door, nor when I close it again.

Finally, I let out the breath I didn't realize I was holding.

Angus and Hunter's door is still closed. They must be asleep.

I pad, barefoot, into the kitchen to start the coffee machine. I spoon ground beans atop the filter, inhaling their toasty, nutty odor. It's a comforting smell. Even before the cafe, coffee was a constant in our parents' household. Without fail, I would wake to the smell of percolating coffee, find mom and dad sitting at the table with steaming mugs in-hand, reading the newspaper together. Dad liked the sports section, while mom favored the front page. The comics section was always set aside for Hunter and me, and we would tussle over it, both wanting to be the first to read *Zits*.

Once the coffee is finished brewing, I pour myself a cup. The only creamer carton in the fridge is soy-based. *Angus' favorite*. I suppose I'll drink mine black; I hate the chalky taste of soy milk. My phone buzzes, making me jump. I'm still on edge. After all, all that stands between me and a bloodthirsty wolf is a closed door. It would snap like kindling if she so much as touched it.

[Hunter: Can you come to the cafe? Insurance needs us to take inventory, see what needs replaced.]

Hunter. I thought he was still asleep. I tap a quick response.

[Candy: On my way]

Then, I pour my coffee into a travel mug. I should tell Haley where I'm going, but I'm too scared to shake her furred shoulder. All I can picture is a flash of teeth, a sunspot of pain before the darkness comes.

CHAPTER TWENTY-SIX
(LEIGH)

———◁◆▷———

I watch Hunter's car pull up to a meter, not quite aligning with the curb. The lithe human unfolds himself from the driver's seat, lurching toward the police cordon like a flung marionette. He ducks under the fluorescent yellow tape, nearly jogging toward the cafe. His sister emerges from the car a minute later, her lips pressed together so firmly they almost seem to disappear.

When I am sure they won't turn back, I walk across the street, peering into the windows. Then suddenly, there's a rectangle of light on the driver's seat. It's an iPhone, the wallpaper a selfie of Angus and Hunter, their smiles wide and blindingly white. I'm not sure I've ever seen Angus smile like that before.

I try the door handle, expecting it to be locked. But in their haste, neither Hunter nor Candy pushed the button on the key fob.

I open the door, taking the phone and pocketing it. This will come in handy.

I scroll through Hunter's camera roll, examining the life he and Angus have created in James' absence. There are a lot of photos of latte art, beach sunsets taken from their back deck, some with the houseboat moored on the dock, and selfies with the cafe as their backdrop. I recognize Renee, the barista, her hair now shorn so short she resembles Mia Farrow—that is, if the actress didn't have access to a hairbrush or a bit of styling mousse.

I find photos of Hunter's sister, her mascara thick and clumpy, but framing gorgeous chocolate-colored eyes. What was her name again? Lolly? Jujubee? *Something* twee and sugary sweet, I think.

I swipe at the screen, again and again, feeling the muscles in my jaw ratchet tighter and tighter. My teeth hurt. This is a world they've created from bloodshed, on the back of my brother's mangled corpse.

"Hunter?" The front door of the cafe opens, the bell above the frame jangling. It's Hunter's sister, right on schedule. She locks the door behind her. With the light streaming through the window, she looks ethereal, otherworldly. Her skin is rose-colored, her auburn hair, tied into a loose chignon, surrounded by a flaming halo of stray baby hairs.

The woman heads toward the back room. She hasn't spotted me behind the counter, sitting next to the pastry case. As soon as her hand rests on the double door, swinging loosely on its hinges, I chirp, "Good morning."

She shrieks in surprise, dropping her phone and wallet. The phone skitters under a nearby table. "We're closed!" she squeaks.

I clamber to my feet, brushing imaginary dust off my jeans. "I figured," I reply, "what with the fire and everything."

"You can't be in here," she insists.

"Your name is *Candy*, right?" I step around the counter, approaching the other woman. It had just come to me: Candy. *How unfortunate.*

Candy dips down and grabs her wallet. "This is private property."

"Someone should have locked the back door then," I reply. "It was basically an invitation."

Candy takes a step back, presumably searching the ground for her missing phone. "Where's Hunter?" she asks. She's frightened. I can smell it on her. She's sweating, the smell sour even in the smoke-stained cafe. But beneath it, there is the smell of meat, which I've come to associate with a full belly and serotonin flooding my brain.

I hold up Hunter's phone. "Asleep, I imagine. I should probably introduce myself. I'm Leigh Volkov."

Candy's face pales. She knows who I am—what I am. At least, she has the sense to be frightened of me. "I'll scream," she stammers. "This street is full of people."

"I'll crush your windpipe before you make a sound." I laugh. There's a table between her and I. She's been inching around it, her fingers on its curvilinear edge.

"Look, I'm really sorry your brother died. My mom died a few years ago. I understand your—"

I bare my teeth at her, feeling them grow sharp in my mouth. "You couldn't possibly understand. James was murdered. Angus and your pathetic brother *murdered* him."

Suddenly, Candy bolts, heading back toward the front door. Fur trickles down my back as I pull myself up onto the cafe table. It's unsteady beneath my sneakered feet. The stitching on my shoes bursts as my feet grow far too large for them, the sharp, curved talons on my toes tapping on the tabletop. As soon as the muscles on my legs grow thick and strong, I leap, catching Candy around the middle just as her fingers alight on the doorknob.

I squeeze her against my barrel chest, and she squirms, kicking me squarely in the ribs. It hurts. Agitated, I grab a fistful of her hair, slamming her forehead against the doorframe. Her skull makes a hollow *thunk*, and her body grows heavy and loose. When I release her, she slumps to the floor, arms, and legs akimbo. A goose egg appears on her forehead, a sunspot of smeared blood at its summit.

"Shit," I breathe. *I've killed her. This wasn't the plan.*

CHAPTER TWENTY-SEVEN
(ANGUS)

—◁◆▷—

My phone vibrates on the end table, and I groan, tucking my chin into Hunter's shoulder. I slept fitfully, a large wolf stalking me doggedly through every conceivable dreamscape. Even the most archetypal dream—standing in the hospital lab, naked, realizing I never actually got my phlebotomy license—starred the wolf. He unabashedly stared as I covered my nakedness with a clipboard, stammering apologies to stunned colleagues. Then, he laughed like a hyena, his pink tongue lolling out of his mouth.

I can still hear him laughing, and I hate the sound clenches my stomach. I used to adore James' laugh. He would always throw his head back, slap at his knee. He chortled with wild abandon, and when you were in on the joke, it felt wonderful.

My phone vibrates again. Carefully, so as not to wake him, I untangle my limbs from Hunter's. My phone has two notifications, both from Hunter's phone.

[Hunter: Come to the cafe. Alone.]

The second is a photo. It's a close-up of Candy's wan face, her eyes closed and her chapped lips slightly parted. There's a huge lump on her temple, a trickle of blood edging down her brow bone. I can see a hand gripping her chin, the nails painted in a smoky grey lacquer and several silver rings adorning the fingers. *Leigh.*

"Hunter," I breathe, shaking the sleeping man by his shoulder. "*Hunter.*"

Hunter groans, rubbing at his eyes with his knuckles. "What time is it?" he murmurs.

"Look," I manage, handing him my phone. He stares at the screen, not comprehending.

"Candace? She's asleep, isn't she?" He lurches out of bed, barreling through the door.

I follow him into the living room and notice signs of life: a coffee cup on the kitchen table, a pot half-empty in the machine. I feel uneasy. In the photo, Candy didn't look right. It was as though everything that made her *Candy* had been scrubbed away.

Hunter opens the guest bedroom door without knocking. Haley abruptly sits up, tucking the bedsheets into her armpits. "What's going on?" she asks, alarmed.

"Is Candy here?" Hunter asks, even though the room clearly has only one occupant. He peers into the en-suite bathroom, opens the doors of the closet as though she could be hiding inside.

"She must have already gotten up," Haley replies. "Someone tell me what's happening. You're freaking me out."

Hunter hands her his phone.

Her eyes widen. "Where is she?" She leans close to the phone, her nose an inch from the screen. "She looks—"

Dead.

But I don't want her to say it aloud. If she does, Hunter will splinter before my eyes. "She's at the cafe," I interrupt. "Leigh wants me to come for her."

Haley reaches over the side of the bed and grabs her shirt, then pulls it over her head. "I'm coming with you," she says, resolute. She places the phone on the bedspread, and the three of us stare at the photo taking up the screen.

"I have to go alone. The message was clear," I insist.

"That's not happening," the woman snaps. She gets out of bed, her shirttail just barely covering the curve of her butt. She pays us no mind, pulling on underwear and shorts. Her hands are shaking just slightly, and she briefly fumbles with the button closure before she manages to snap it closed.

"I'm not sitting here," Hunter adds. "My sister is in danger, Angus."

♦ ♦ ♦

I enter the cafe through the heavy back door, left propped open with a chipped cinderblock. The back room is coated in a thin layer of ash, the shelving nearest the trash can a hunk of warped metal. Several of the ceiling tiles had fallen, and it is impossible not to step on them. They *crunch* beneath my feet, fiberglass scraping against the once-polished concrete floor. So much for being inconspicuous.

It reeks, and I pull the neck of my t-shirt up over my nose. My eyes water.

"Who's there?" A voice calls from the cafe's dining room, their voice barely penetrating the heavy double doors. Still, I know that voice. With a pang, I think of nights in the warehouse in Portland, Leigh's persistent knock on the wall between our two bedrooms. *Keep it down, you lovebirds. Some of us have a shift in the morning!* Her voice always sounded like a chipmunk's by the time it leaked through the drywall and ductwork, making James and I laugh.

"It's me, Leigh. Angus." I slowly ease open the double doors, squinting in the sudden light. Compared to the back room, the cafe proper is lustrous, having been largely unaffected by the blaze.

Leigh sits on the counter, her knees crossed. Her shoulders slump, her fingers gripping the counter's edge. She looks unkempt; her clothes rumpled and her hair greasy and limp. Even her eyebrows, which she had religiously shaved off, have started to grow back in bristly patches. "You came alone?" she asks brusquely. Her voice trembles with unfettered emotion, though her eyes are remarkably dry.

"Yes. Where's Candy?" I ask.

Leigh gestures toward the front door. Candy lays in a pool of sunlight, her head resting on the welcome mat Hunter had picked out during the winter months, when customers tracked in mud and slush on their shoes. It's made of braided rubber, a large steaming coffee mug painted on its center.

"Oh my god," I exclaim, rushing to her, falling to my knees. I rest my hand on her shoulder, expecting it to be cold. But it's warm, twitching under my touch. *She's alive.* "Candy?"

Candy's brow furrows, a soft moan escaping her lips. Her eyelids crack open, but squeeze shut again. "Angus?" she manages. Her hair sticks to the nasty, weeping lump on her brow.

"Yeah." I grin, relief pouring through me. "I've come to take you home."

"Always the optimist," Leigh remarks, sliding off the counter. "Surely you realize you aren't walking out of here." Fur spirals up her throat, adorning her cheeks.

I gently lay Candy's head back on the mat, regaining my feet. "Leigh, this isn't you."

"Oh?" She laughs, the sound perverted by her lengthening snout. It sounds like a gargle. "Please tell me all about who I am, *Gus*."

"James *murdered* someone." Paresthesia tickles my mid-back, crawling up my spine. "He killed a man to *eat* him. He attacked me—and Hunter. I acted in self-defense." The seams of my shirtsleeves pop as my body swells, muscle layering on top of corded muscle.

"James deserved *mercy*. He was your *husband*." She shoves aside a cafe table, sending it spinning on its edge. It collides with the bakery case, cracking the glass.

"Were you planning to offer me mercy?" After all, both she and Luka stood by James' side in the end, sunk their teeth into *my* fur. Surely, they wouldn't have allowed me the opportunity to beg for my life.

Leigh lunges, and I brace myself, grunting when she slams her shoulder into my abdomen. I wrap my big arms around her, pinning her against my chest. "I'm so sorry he's gone," I murmur into her ear. "Stop this. I don't want to hurt you."

Her jaws snap on my shoulder, forcing me to release my grip. Then, her claws rake across my snout, leaving bloodless divots behind. "I am going to kill you," she snarls, "and then I'm going to find your pathetic human."

She is quicker and more nimble than I am, and she leaps atop me, trying to press her thumbs into my eyes. I stumble, collide with a table, and blindly grab a fistful of her fur. She yips but doesn't release me. I can feel the tip of her nail puncture the thin tissue just beneath my right eye, and I howl in pain. I can't shake her off. My eye waters, a kaleidoscope of color and blinding light bursting therein. Then, there's nothing, not even darkness.

Suddenly, something slams into us both, knocking us apart. I clap my paw over my weeping eye, protecting it from further attack. Haley, wolfish, stands between the two of us, panting. "Are you okay?" she asks me.

"Get Candy out of here," I tell her.

Haley does as I ask, gingerly scooping the semi-conscious woman into her arms.

Leigh's nostrils flare, her dark eyes flickering between the two of us as if weighing her odds. Despite being outnumbered, she doesn't submit, nor falter. Instead, she lunges at me again, landing a punch on my blind side. Her knuckles connect with my skull, wrenching my neck.

I manage to grasp her muzzle, slamming her head into the brick wall. She kicks me in the ribs, freeing herself from my grasp. Blood trickles down a gash on her cheek, matting her fur. She laces her hands around my neck, squeezing tight.

For a brief moment, I panic. Dark motes crowd what remains of my vision, and then —

Bang.

CHAPTER TWENTY-EIGHT
(HALEY)

———◁◆▷———

I climb the fire escape outside of the cafe, wincing when the rusty metal screams beneath my feet. Angus looks up at me, pressing his finger to his lips.

Sorry, I mouth, trying to step more carefully. I can hear the back door open and close beneath me; Angus is inside, as planned.

The metal is hot on my palms, and I move quickly, desperate to get off the rickety ladder. Dimly, I hear a car door close, and I look to see Hunter at the end of the alley, leaning against the idling car. I can't quite make out his features, but his body language—arms crossed over his chest, shoulders squared—is clear: he's upset for being delegated as the getaway driver.

I push the window open, the pane squealing. I am immediately struck by the overpowering smell of smoke. It makes my eyes water. I squeeze through the window feet-first, landing heavily on my butt. It's dark inside, and the air conditioner is off. The air is stagnant, dust motes dancing in the beams of sunlight offered by the windows. It smells a bit off, and I expect the electricity is off entirely; the foodstuffs in the fridge—takeout containers, mostly—are slowly rotting.

I can't shake the image of Candy's face. I looked at the photo as we drove toward the cafe, as if I could divine anything from it. But Candy's kidnapper was careful, cropping it tight on her face, the large head wound taking precedence. I found myself looking at her eyes, the lids closed and slightly crinkled. Was she unconscious, dead, or simply mid-blink? I looked at it with such ferocity it replaced the image of Candy that had preceded it: the pink-cheeked woman who kissed my thighs, ran her hands through my fur. Every time I tried to conjure it—her soft hands, her lips trailing down my shoulder—I only see her grey skin, the rivulet of blood trickling down her cheek and into her mouth, painting her lips red.

I cross the loft, easing open the front door. The stairwell below is dark, and I can't help but picture a horror movie monster spidering up the stairs. I shiver but press onward, using the bannister as my guide. It's as quiet as a tomb, and every squeak or scuff of my sneakers is akin to a thunderclap. Near the bottom, I see a large rectangle of light, and I push it with my palms. It's the door leading into the cafe's back room.

There's no sign of Angus. It smells strongly of smoke here, and there's a moldy dampness too. The floor is wet, either from the fire hoses or a leak somewhere. The L-shaped kitchen area consists of a basin sink, a workspace, and a large commercial oven, is difficult to navigate. A cooling rack had been upended, and I have to scamper over it; it's too heavy to move.

Suddenly, I hear Angus' rumbling voice. He's in the dining area, through a pair of double doors just up ahead. There's a circular window on the door, akin to a porthole, and I stand on my tiptoes to peer through it. Angus is in mid-transformation, a horrific amalgamation of wolf and man. A table rolls on its side across the floor, crashing into the bakery case with a muffled crash.

A wolf—presumably Leigh—leaps at Angus, and the two snarl and bite at one another. Angus is being careful; it's apparent he's trying not to injure her. But his caution is leaving him open to attack, and Leigh is taking advantage of it. She presses her thumbs into his eye sockets, her lips pulled back into a gruesome sneer. Angus' legs buckle, and the she-wolf looms over him, pressing her whole weight into his orbital cavity. I can't help but to imagine his eye bursting like a grape, the fluid inside trickling down his cheek like tears.

I have to help him. But—

I'm frightened.

The first snap of my clavicle is like being doused in icy water. A shiver of horror trickles down my quickly lengthening spine. My teeth crowd my mouth, and my tongue swells. My sensitive taste buds prickle, and I am keenly aware of a coppery taste in my mouth. I've been anxiously chewing the inside of my cheek, and it's bled slightly. Saliva pools in my mouth.

My stomach clenches tight. The wolf is hungry. Distantly, I can smell meat, blood, and something *human*. At first, that revelation makes me feel heady, needful. But then, I realize…it's Candy's smell, and the blood is fresh. *She's alive!*

I barrel through the double doors, slamming into the two wolves.

Angus looks at me through one eye, the other hidden beneath his enormous paw. "Get Candy out of here," he orders.

Candy is laying on the doormat, curled up in the fetal position. She looks horribly small, like an abandoned kitten left in a cardboard box. Carefully, I gather her into my arms. I try very hard not to inhale the smell of her, to ignore the way my salivary glands contract at the very thought of licking the blood off her forehead.

Candy's eyelids crack open, and her lips part. "Hale," she breathes. Her cheek, wet with blood and tears, rests against my breast.

"I've got you," I murmur.

The corners of her lips twitch into a tiny smile.

Leigh and Angus clash again, and I hesitate. The plan was for me to get Candy and get her out to the car. Angus would take care of Leigh, but she clearly has the upper hand. The she-wolf wraps her claws around the Alpha wolf's throat, and his eyes bulge. His ruined eye—bloodshot, the pupil blown out—rolls in its socket.

Bang!

Tiny shards of shattered glass fill the air, raining down on me as I wrap myself around Candy. I can feel them tear into my skin, creating hundreds of tiny lacerations. *What's happening?* It's as though the cafe imploded. I slowly straighten up, turning to see the ruined front end of Hunter's Camry, now half-inside the cafe. The engine smokes, making the air appear hazy. It's difficult to see.

The driver's side door opens, and Hunter steps out, his nose bleeding profusely. He's nearly as pale as his sister. "Angus?" he calls, his voice wobbling and plaintive.

A bit of debris—a triangular-shaped remnant of the door, an overturned table, and two chairs, their legs interlocked—shifts, and the enormous wolf regains his feet. "I told you to wait in the car," he manages before falling to his knees.

"I did," Hunter deadpanx as he rushes to his lover's side, stroking his fur with shaking hands. "Are you alright?"

But I don't catch the rest of their conversation. The cuprous smell of blood fills my nostrils, and I look for the source. Leigh is laying on the linoleum, human now, her body wedged beneath the car. Her eyes— wide, unblinking—stare at nothing in particular.

CHAPTER TWENTY-NINE
(CANDY)

—◁◆▷—

"We're going to be late," Haley badgers, meeting my eyes in the mirror's reflection. I raise my eyebrows, patting more powder onto my forehead, trying in vain to cover the purplish bruise there.

"Nearly done," I say.

Haley presses her lips against my cheek, her lipstick leaving a pink smudge on my skin. "You look perfect," she assures me. "You always do."

"I just—" I sigh, leaning into her warmth. "I just want to look into the mirror and see Candy—*normal* Candy." Normalcy seems like a pipe dream now, unattainable. I went to class hoping to find it in a seminar on F. Scott Fitzgerald. After all, it was the most ordinary thing I could think of doing. But instead, I left midway through, tired of being stared at by my classmates. Whispers followed me out into the hall.

With the cafe closed, I've spent most of my time at Hunter's bungalow. We are all still nursing our wounds, both visible and invisible. Angus bumps into the furniture, still growing accustomed to his eyepatch. Hunter is quiet, withdrawn. He sleeps fitfully, often waking us when he trundles into the living room to watch late night infomercials with the volume too loud.

"Come on," Haley wheedles. "Angus and Hunter already left."

I rise from the edge of the bed, setting aside the handheld mirror. Haley looks beautiful in a knee-length skirt and a high-necked blouse. I can't help but touch her, running my fingertips down her naked arms. Her lips part, her breath hot on my face. "You look beautiful," I tell her.

"You dressed me," she reminds me. "This is all your doing." She's right and half the closet's contents litter the bed as a result. I made her try on several out-fits before I decided on this one. It's elegant, albeit understated — perfect for a birthday party.

I wish we could stay here. The house is quiet, and it's as though we are the only two people in the entire world. We've hardly had a moment alone. "Can't we just send a gift?" I wheedle, wrapping my arms around her tapered waist.

"You know we can't." Still, Haley's hands slip underneath my shift dress, running up my thighs. She kisses me softly. Haley is always so careful when she touches me, as though I'll shatter in her hands. She's not entirely wrong. I've felt so fragile since that morning in the cafe. She fills her palms with me, squeezing my ass. "Though, we have a few minutes, if we walk *very quickly*."

"We'll run," I murmur, imagining running down the gravel road in my bare feet, my heels dangling from my fingertips. Gently, Haley lays me back on the mattress, atop the pile of clothes. Her eyes flash, a glimmer of the wolfishness threatening to spill forth. But I'm not frightened. She hesitates, her hands alighting on my knobby knees. "Hale," I murmur, an assurance. *I trust you.*

I want you.

Haley shucks my skirt around my hips, revealing the triangle of my underwear. Her mouth descends onto the tops of my thighs. She scrapes her squarish teeth along my skin, making me mewl.

I raise my hips as if to say, *please.*

CHAPTER THIRTY
(HALEY)

———◁◆▷———

"You have some lipstick just *there*," Candy says, wiping away the spot on my neck with her saliva-dampened thumb.

I snicker, any number of cutesy responses ready to launch off my tongue. But my nervousness has stolen my voice.

This is my first time at Ama Chilton's house. She intimidates me; I feel flayed open when she looks into my eyes, and I am certain she can divine my future just by examining a coil of intestine. Even Candy seems affected by the centenarian's inherent power. *She's scary*, Candy confided on our walk over. *Even when she talks softly, I feel like I'm being yelled at.*

The sun beats down on the porch, and I can feel sweat pool on my lower back. "Are you going to knock?" Candy asks.

"Are you?" I counter.

Candy sighs and raps her knuckles against the door. When it opens, we are greeted by Toby, who is wearing a pale yellow sundress that, with her pregnant belly, makes her look like a lemon. "Hey," she says cheerily. "Come on in."

The bungalow is full of sunlight, and it's somewhat stifling save for the cool sea air coming through the open sliding glass door. I can see Hunter on the deck, wearing khaki shorts and a pair of ugly Birkenstock sandals. He has a drink glass in hand, something fluorescent orange on ice therein. He's talking to Alexandre, and for the moment, he looks relaxed. It's a far cry from the sullen insomniac who haunts our bungalow.

Angus sits at the kitchen table, drinking a beer. His diminutive grandmother sits at his right, her wrinkled hands wrapped around a highball glass. Except, instead of a cocktail, it's filled with ice water, a sprig of mint wilting against the rim. "We were just trying to convince Ama to tell us about the old days," Toby says. "Y'know, back when there were horse n' buggies."

Angus guffaws. His eyepatch makes him look roguish, and it suits him. Candy excuses herself to go see her brother, but I stay, sinking into one of the Queen Anne style chairs. Maybe Ama will tell me more about my grandfather, the affliction we share.

"I've lived a long time," Ama says with a barking laugh. "But not quite that long."

Toby sits too, reaching for a bag of potato chips on the tabletop. The bag crinkles loudly as she grabs a handful of cheddar and sour cream Ruffles. "Tell us about Rafe. I love hearing you talk about him. It's almost as romantic as *The Notebook*."

I know that name. "He was my grandfather's friend," I remark.

Ama smiles, the gesture causing her wrinkles to deepen into veritable canyons. "Samuel and Rafe were the best of friends, especially 'round the time Angus' mama was born. We had daughters around the same time. I expect Cordelia Campbell is your mama, right?"

"Yes," I reply. I feel strangely breathless. I had been trying very hard not to think about mom, Tennessee, *Tara*.

"Toby just likes to hear about Rafe and I falling in love," Ama says. "Can you fetch me the photo album? The one I showed you a few weeks ago?" she asks Angus, who rises to do as requested. When he returns, he places the large tome before her as though it's a priceless relic.

With slender fingers, she opens the leatherbound book, touching the plastic lined pages reverently. "Look," she says, shifting the book so I can see. "This was your grandfather back in 1949."

Samuel Campbell grins up at me, his arm draped around an angular woman. "That's your grandmother. Nadia. She was a human, you know," Ama adds.

"I know. She was pregnant with my Uncle Henry before they got married." I lean close to the photo, examining my grandfather's face. He looks genuinely happy, carefree. He certainly doesn't look haunted by his own rabid nature. I twist in my chair, looking at Candy. On the deck, her hair windblown, she laughs, clasping her brother's shoulder. Even Hunter's lip upturns into some semblance of a grin. She must feel my eyes on her because she turns to look at me, quirking her eyebrow. I look back at the photo album, my cheeks hot.

"They were married for forty long years. Much longer than Rafe and I got." Ama twists a gold band around her ring finger. It's plain, discolored and tarnished.

"She died when I was a baby," I reply. "I've only ever seen her photo."

"Surely, he spoke of her. He was a man obsessed. His letters—his phone calls—were mostly long accounts of what wonderful thing Nadia was up to. She was a schoolteacher but also the bookkeeper for his garage."

He hadn't. Or rather, I hadn't given him the time of day. I was too angry, too mired in my own discomfort. All I have is the man illustrated in his journals, a man who was a far cry from the decent soul Ama knew. "We didn't speak," I remind her.

Ama flips a page, revealing a group of photos. They are in color, taken just outside of this very bungalow. Ama is wearing an ivory dress, with a plunging sweetheart neckline and a full, poufy skirt. She's barefoot, laughing. Another woman, who I don't recognize, holds her shoes aloft, her crimson mouth agape as if mid-shout. Nadia is there, too, wearing a rayon party dress, one of the straps falling off her shoulder. She's laughing, too, bent at the waist with her arms wrapped around her stomach.

"What was so funny?" Toby asks.

"You can't tell but I was very pregnant here," Ama chuckles. "My shoes didn't fit because my feet were too swollen. I ended up getting married barefoot, hopping from foot to foot because the sand was so damn hot."

The next photo is of Ama and a tall, lithe man. His face is serious, and he's wearing Navy dress blues, a smattering of medals adorning his chest. "Rafe!" Toby exclaims. "What a dreamboat."

He resembles Angus; both men have sharp jawlines and dark hair. However, Rafe's eyes are ocher, rather than the shocking aquamarine Angus inherited from his grandmother.

"What happened to him?" I ask.

"A heart attack," Ama murmurs. "Just seven years after we were married. Sam was a pallbearer. He dug the grave by hand, too, along with some of Rafe's Navy buddies."

"I wish," I begin, the words lodging in my throat. "I wish I had known him—my grandfather. I had twenty-eight years with him, and I squandered it."

"Anger and resentment are powerful emotions," Angus says. "I think we all felt that this week." We all grow silent, thinking of the limp, heavy she-wolf we carried out the back of Ebb and Flow, hurrying as the pall of sirens grew nearer. Only Hunter remained behind, ready to weave a tale regarding a faulty brake pedal.

We brought her here, to Ama's bungalow, wrapping her up inside a clean bedspread we laid out upon the floor. Angus sat on the drooping couch, his hands teepeed beneath his bearded chin, staring at the woman. He wept, unabashedly, and then, when the sun set, he carried her out into the forest to bury.

I trace the wood grain on the tabletop. "I'm tired of being angry." I truly am. Maybe, I think, if I accept my skin—fur and all—I can contend with the hunger.

Maybe, it will abate. It had for Sam. There was no miracle cure, it seemed, just a man finding something akin to a family.

"Run with us tonight," Ama says, "after we cut the cake."

And I do.

Candy folds my clothes over her arm, running a hand along my silky haunch. "Come home to me," she says.

I lope between the two white wolves, the old Frenchmen taking up the rear, and when my paws touch sand, I feel as though I'm flying.

EPILOGUE
(CANDY)

————◁◆▷————

"It's done," I announce, closing my laptop. My dry eyes ache, and when I glance at the clock, I am startled to find it is well past midnight.

Hunter startles. He'd been dozing on the couch beside me, having drank more than his fair share of Cosmopolitans at the party. "Wha—" he mutters, stretching. He looks for Angus and Haley, but they aren't back from their run yet.

"It's just a poem," I tell him. "But it's a start. Maybe I'm finally getting past my writer's block."

"Can I read it?" He scoots closer to me. I open the laptop, tilting the screen so he can see the document. He reads the short stanzas aloud, adopting the cadence of a poet in a coffeehouse:

> We were all wild once.
> Desperate, scrabbling,
> searching for the scent trail
> of mushrooms safe to eat,
> or grouse eggs hidden in

207

leafy bowls.
Our stomachs twisting,
tighter than the braids
in our horse's manes.
Hunger is the great equalizer.
But—
Some of us are wolves,
and the earth speaks to us,
telling us where to look for
whitetail, horned stag,
the clearest stream.

When he is finished, Hunter is quiet for a long time. He stares at the screen, and I can see the words reflected in his eyes.

"You know," he says, "sometimes I think about it too, what it must be like for them." He puts the laptop aside, resting his elbows on his knees. "I think, I think it's something I want."

ABOUT THE AUTHOR
BEAU LAKE

---◁◆▷---

B eau Lake is a tattooed, blue-haired, queer romance writer skulking around the mountains of Virginia. She is very happily married and lives with a menagerie of children (2), dogs (3), and plants.

Her current hobbies include digital art, social/ animal activism, and screaming into the void. Mostly the latter. She is passionate about ending greyhound racing in the United States and worldwide, and shares her home with a retired racer named River. Other favorite activities include listening to true crime podcasts, staring at empty Word documents while having existential crises, and asking herself "What Would Stephen King Do?"

Beau writes both traditional and horror/supernatural LGBTQIA romance. Werewolves are her favorite because they have sharp teeth and even sharper personalities.

Some of her published work includes the well-received DC Pride series, co-written with Tatum West

(Proud, Out, and The Space Between Us). The Wolves of Wharton is her first supernatural series, with more to come!

She can be found online via Facebook, Twitter, or at authorbeaulake.com. She loves t3alking with readers and can be reached at authorbeaulake@gmail. com. Vegetarian recipes are also appreciated.

facebook.com/beau.lake.77

facebook.com/groups/1813967932089935
Twitter @beau__lakebeaulakebooks.com

OTHER BOOKS

Co-authored w/ Tatum West:
Proud, Out, The Space Between Us

BY BEAU LAKE:

The Beast Beside Me
The Beast Within Me
Taming the Beast
The Beast After Me
Charming the Beast
The Beast Like Me

4 Horsemen Publications

Romance

Ann Shepphird
The War Council

Emily Bunney
All or Nothing
All the Way
All Night Long
All She Needs
Having it All
All at Once
All Together
All for Her

Lynn Chantale
The Baker's Touch
Blind Secrets

Mimi Francis
Private Lives
Second Chances
Run Away Home
The Professor

Fantasy & Paranormal Romance

Beau Lake
The Beast Beside Me
The Beast Within Me
The Beast After Me
The Beast Like Me
An Eye for Emeralds
Swimming in Sapphires
Pining for Pearls

D. Lambert
To Walk into the Sands
Rydan
Northlander
Esparan
King
Traitor
His Last Name

J.M. Paquette
Klauden's Ring
Solyn's Body
The Inbetween
Hannah's Heart
Call Me Forth
Invite Me In

Lyre R. Saenz
Prelude
Falsetto in the Woods
Ragtime Swing
Sonata
Song of the Sea
The Devil's Trill
Bercuese

To Heal a Songbird
Ghost March
Nocturne

Valerie Willis
Cedric: The Demonic Knight
Romasanta: Father of
Werewolves
The Oracle: Keeper of the
Gaea's Gate
Artemis: Eye of Gaea
King Incubus: A New Reign

V.C. Willis
Prince's Priest
Priest's Assassin

Young Adult Fantasy

Blaise Ramsay
Through The Black Mirror
The City of Nightmares
The Astral Tower
The Lost Book of
the Old Blood
Shadow of the Dark Witch
Chamber of the Dead God

C.R. Rice
Denial
Anger
Bargaining
Depression
Acceptance
Broken Beginnings:
Story of Thane
Shattered Start: Story of Sera
Sins of The Father:
Story of Silas
Honorable Darkness: Story of
Hex and Snip
A Love Lost: Story of Radnar

4HorsemenPublications.com